cheesecake

The Core of an Onion: Peeling the Rarest Common Food
The Unreasonable Virtue of Fly Fishing
Salmon: A Fish, the Earth, and the History of Their Common Fate
Milk! A 10,000-Year Food Fracas
Havana: A Subtropical Delirium
Paper: Paging Through History
International Night: A Father and Daughter Cook Their Way
Around the World
Ready for a Brand New Beat: How "Dancing in the Street" Became
the Anthem for a Changing America
Birdseye: The Adventures of a Curious Man
Hank Greenberg: The Hero Who Didn't Want to Be One
What? Are These the 20 Most Important Questions in Human
History—or Is This a Game of 20 Questions?
The Eastern Stars: How Baseball Changed the Dominican Town of
San Pedro de Macoris
The Food of a Younger Land: A Portrait of American Food . . . from
the Lost WPA Files
The Last Fish Tale: The Fate of the Atlantic and Survival in
Gloucester, America's Oldest Fishing Port and Most Original Town
The Big Oyster: History on the Half Shell
Non-violence: The History of a Dangerous Idea
1968: The Year That Rocked the World

FICTION

City Beasts: Fourteen Short Stories of Uninvited Wildlife
Battle Fatigue
Edible Stories: A Novel in Sixteen Parts
Boogaloo on 2nd Avenue: A Novel of Pastry, Guilt, and Music
The White Man in the Tree and Other Stories

CHEESECAKE

A NOVEL

MARK KURLANSKY

BLOOMSBURY PUBLISHING
NEW YORK · LONDON · OXFORD · NEW DELHI · SYDNEY

BLOOMSBURY PUBLISHING
Bloomsbury Publishing Inc.
1359 Broadway, New York, NY 10018, USA
50 Bedford Square, London, WC1B 3DP, UK
Bloomsbury Publishing Ireland Limited,
29 Earlsfort Terrace, Dublin 2, D02 AY28, IRELAND

BLOOMSBURY, BLOOMSBURY PUBLISHING, and the Diana logo are
trademarks of Bloomsbury Publishing Plc

First published in the United States 2025
Copyright © Mark Kurlansky, 2025

ISBN: HB: 978-1-63973-572-3; EBOOK: 978-1-63973-573-0

LIBRARY OF CONGRESS CATALOGING-IN-PUBLICATION DATA IS AVAILABLE

2 4 6 8 10 9 7 5 3 1

Typeset by Westchester Publishing Services

Printed in the United States by Lakeside Book Company,
Harrisonburg, VA

To find out more about our authors and books visit www.bloomsbury.com
and sign up for our newsletters.

Bloomsbury books may be purchased for business or promotional use.
For information on bulk purchases please contact Macmillan Corporate and
Premium Sales Department at specialmarkets@macmillan.com.
For product safety related questions contact productsafety@bloomsbury.com.

For Marian, Talia, our neighbors, and their dogs

*Those who are serious in ridiculous matters
will be ridiculous in serious matters.*

—CATO THE ELDER

A party without cake is really just a meeting.

—JULIA CHILD

CONTENTS

INTRODUCTION:
COULD CATO BE A WEST SIDER?

I despise recipes that promise results without work,
or success without technique.

—ROBERT FARRAR CAPON, *THE SUPPER OF THE LAMB*

By the late twentieth century, introducing cheesecake to New York made as much sense as introducing baked beans to Boston.

In 1929 Arnold Reuben, a German Jew living on the Upper West Side of Manhattan, started making cheesecake with cream cheese, another New York invention dating back to the 1870s. In the 1880s its creators branded it "Philadelphia Cream Cheese," a marketing ploy—that part of Pennsylvania had a reputation for high-quality dairy farms—but even Philadelphia cream cheese was made in New York. By using cream cheese, Reuben redefined New York cheesecake, seemingly forever. This was all well established until Cato came to town.

Marcus Porcius Cato, a Roman commonly referred to simply as Cato the Elder, lived from 234 to 149 BCE. From an agricultural background, he opposed what he saw as a growing tendency toward excessive luxury in Roman society. Could anyone be more ill-suited to Manhattan's liberal Upper West Side today?

He was one of Rome's most right-wing politicians, the kind of figure who could not get elected dog catcher on the Upper West Side (if such a position, God forbid, existed in the neighborhood). But more than two thousand years ago, Cato did something that had never been done before: He published a recipe. Once a recipe is published there's no telling where it will go. It may live forever. Roman senators may not be immortal, but recipes can be.

Noted for his oratory skills, Cato attacked other important Roman figures for their corruption. He was also an unabashed proponent of harsh treatment for slaves, servants, and wives. He railed against women and women's rights. According to the Roman biographer Plutarch, he also abused animals, which is about as low as you can get on the Upper West Side.

Cato was associated with the second and third Punic Wars, bitter struggles against the North African nation of Carthage. He fought with distinction in the Second Punic War. Arguing for a third war because Carthage was being rebuilt, he presented the Senate with a handful of figs, according to Plutarch (or, according to Pliny, a single fig). He pointed out that this succulent, plump fruit had been picked in Carthage only two days earlier—that was how close their enemy was—and argued for a third Punic War to completely destroy Carthage. He got his wish, and the ensuing campaign became one of the most ruthless in all of Rome's brutal history.

Only one likeness of Cato has survived: a marble bust, a work that portrays his face with an especially cruel expression. According to Plutarch, Cato once said, "After I'm dead I'd rather have people ask why I have no monument than why I have one." But what they have ended up asking, at least on the Upper West Side, is *how does his cheesecake recipe work?*

Like many right-wingers, Cato was extremely nationalistic, a true xenophobe who didn't think Rome was nearly Roman enough. He especially disliked Greeks and Greek influence, which is ironic since some historians think that Greeks were the first cheesecake makers, as they are on Eighty-Sixth Street in my story. But the ancient Greeks left behind no recipes for posterity, only cheese molds.

It was a matter of particular irritation to Cato that the literature of Rome was all written in Greek. So he invented Latin literature, writing numerous books in Latin, though perhaps he was not one of its greatest practitioners. We don't know because only one of his several books has survived: *De Agricultura* (*On Farming*), written in 160 BCE.

Aside from being the oldest surviving example of Latin prose, it is not a terribly notable book. It does not have Plutarch's historical insights, Martial's wit, nor Seneca's reflections on life, and it certainly does not have the lyricism of the three greats—Ovid, Horace, and Virgil. So it goes. The first automobiles were not the best either. *De Agricultura* simply contains advice on buying and maintaining a farm. But wedged between advice on how to organize the land, raise livestock, and beat and starve slaves, there are recipes. This makes it the oldest cookbook in existence. "Book" is the key word here, because more than a thousand years earlier, the Sumerians wrote recipes on clay tablets. Those we've recovered were mostly for stews—certainly not for cheesecake.

Cato's recipes are few. There are brief instructions for how to make mustacei, a simple dish of soft fresh cheese with lard and must, or unfermented wine juice:

> Prepare mustacei thus: Moisten a modius (two gallons, a peck or a half bushel) of fine flour with must. Add anise, cumin, two pounds of fat, 1 pound of cheese, and a grated bay twig. When you have shaped them, place bay leaves beneath and cook.

It seems cheesecake was eaten in Cato's Rome because he offers two cheesecake recipes. The less interesting one, savillum, is a simpler, perhaps earlier version. A half pound of flour is mixed with two and a half pounds of cheese (he doesn't say what kind of flour nor what kind of cheese). It is mixed with an egg and honey and baked in an earthenware dish. After baking it is covered with honey and sprinkled with poppyseed—easy enough to make, but not very intriguing. Perhaps this was the ordinary version of Roman cheesecake. But the crowning recipe, the one culinary historians have been trying to decipher for centuries, is the one he called "placenta," a perplexing recipe for cheesecake also using cheese and honey. Ironically Cato's label, placenta, meaning flatcake, comes from a Greek word *plakoeis*. The placenta recipe is lengthy, detailed, and incomprehensible. It cannot be exactly followed without producing something that is extremely unappealing—and even then, some guess-work is involved. Some historians think it was meant not to be eaten but used for religious ceremonies, for which it would be burned. But others believe it was a dish intended for feasts. Cato famously loved to host large feasts, despite his custom of denouncing Roman extravagance. Some think it was a sweet since it called for honey, but it still may have been a savory dish. Where in a meal, if at all, was it served? And the fresh sheep's cheese he mentions—what is it? Is it soft or hard? It must be brined since it has to be soaked. And the dough he calls "tracta," which historians think is a fore-runner of pasta, would not come together in the recipe as he writes it. It would be impossibly tough. Did he forget to mention that you have to boil it? The recipe requires research. It calls for emmer (*Triticum dicoccum*) groats, a common flour in Cato's day that was parched and pounded. What is the modern equivalent?

Why is this recipe so ambiguous? Was it because he did not make it himself? He would not have written the recipe himself either, of course, but would have dictated it to a scribe, which was the custom at the time. But Cato was not kitchen shy. Plutarch tells us that he liked to get involved in the preparation of foods. Was this cake never really made? Or was Cato not good at writing recipes? Cato hated frivolity—he denounced philosophy as too frivolous—and so we can assume that he found nothing frivolous about the idea of writing a cookbook.

The first Roman cookbook that consisted purely of recipes was published almost two centuries later and attributed to Marcus Gavius Apicius, a popular figure in food history who serves as a cautionary tale for gourmands. Apicius loved exotic dishes and killed himself because his dwindling inheritance was no longer enough to buy the ingredients that would satisfy his appetite. Unfortunately he did the deed shortly before "Apicius's cookbook" came out, so the true author, or probably authors, are unknown. In any event, his recipes were written in spoken rather than classical Latin.

Remember, Cato had been the first, and possibly the only, writer to record recipes in classical Latin. Maybe it wasn't a great language for recipe writing. Scribes in Cato's age were not accustomed to writing Latin prose of any kind.

Was there some miscommunication between the cook, Cato, and the scribe? Or was the problem that the staff hated Cato? Quite possibly, given his views on the treatments of underlings, the scribe (and more especially the baker) would've loathed him and been uninterested in aiding his pet project.

Here is Cato's recipe. You can try it for yourself, or see what a number of people on West Eighty-Sixth Street who, like Cato, were given to hosting feasts, did with it.

Make placenta this way: two pounds bread-wheat flour to make the base; four pounds flour and two pounds emmer groats to make tracta, turn the emmer into water; when it is really soft, turn into a mixing bowl and drain well; then knead it with your hands. When it is well worked, add the four pounds flour gradually and make into sheets. Arrange them in a basket to dry out.

When they are dry, rearrange them neatly. In making each sheet after you have kneaded them, press them with a cloth soaked in oil, wipe them round, and dampen them.

When they are made, heat up your cooking fire and your crock, then moisten the two pounds of flour and knead it: from this you make a thin base.

Put in water, 14 pounds sheep's milk, not sour, quite fresh. Let it steep, changing the water three times. Take it out and gradually squeeze it dry with the hands. When all the cheese is properly dried out, in a clean mixing bowl knead it with the hands, breaking it down as much as possible. Then take a clean flour sieve and press the cheese through the sieve into the bowl. Then take four and a half pounds of good honey and mix it well with the cheese.

Then put the base on a clean table that has a foot of space with oiled bay leaves under it, and make the placenta.

First put a single sheet over the whole base, then one by one, with the mixture and add them spreading in such a way that you eventually use up all the cheese and honey. On the top, put one more sheet by itself. Then draw up the edges of the base having previously stoked up the fire; then place the placenta to cook, cover it with the heated crock, and put hot coals around and above it.

Be sure to cook it well and slowly. Open to check on it two or three times. When it is cooked, remove it and coat in honey. This makes a one-gallon placenta.

The Second Assimilation

By the late 1980s, the Katsikases were in the throes of their second assimilation. The first had come in the 1970s, when New York was doing so badly it seemed up for grabs, so the Katsikases left their small rock-bound Greek island and came to grab it. Far from those rough, round boulders that once defined them, Nikodemos had become Niki. His brother Achilles had become Art. But Niki's wife, Adara, had refused to be Ana. That was all right. Niki and Art didn't believe assimilation was as important for women.

They found a house in Queens—not large but big enough for now. It seemed surprisingly inexpensive for New York. They were in a woodland residence that only recently had been built up, with houses sprouting like wayward dandelions over all the open space. They had various sidings, like they were wearing costumes—some looked like stone, some brick, some wood—but they were all sheet metal. To squeeze in as many houses as possible, they were all built shoulder to shoulder, like trees in an orchard whose planter hadn't allowed enough room for growth. The Katsikases had seen olive groves like this back home and knew they were never productive. Despite the crowding, everybody in their new neighborhood had a deep backyard surrounded by trees for privacy. They were imitation suburbanites.

The Katsikases had moved to New York to run a Greek diner. Back home they had been told diners made for good business in New York. They had always been certain theirs should be in Manhattan, but when they arrived, they found that their home was an hour from the island by car. By subway it took even longer, with one or two transfers. How could they be in New York and still be so far away from the city? Back on their Greek island they could take a cart to the port, get on a white-and-blue ferry, and be on another island in less time.

Still, the Katsikases weren't deterred. Upon landing in Queens, they began to evaluate Manhattan's neighborhoods for their restaurant. Unlike in Greece, property value was not a question of rainfall, cloud cover, southern exposure, or the rockiness or chalkiness of the soil. So what was it a question of? The amount of sidewalk traffic? The clothes that people in the neighborhood wore? Whether there were lines for subways or buses, or whether most people took taxis?

Art, who was certain he had greater expertise than his brother and sister-in-law, announced that while the Upper West Side was not the best neighborhood in Manhattan, it was affordable and had real potential. What did "real potential" mean? There were a lot of Jews in the neighborhood. That was a good sign. Before the Katsikases left for America,

Art's friend in Athens, Calix, who had been to America two times, had given him advice: "In New York, always follow the Jews."

So, because their home in Queens was so easy on their budget, they were able to rent a small commercial space on a good corner of West Eighty-Sixth Street. The Katsikases decided to call their restaurant the Katz Brothers, even though everyone knew it was Greek. They thought Katz would be a better name for the neighborhood. "The Katsikases" certainly would not work. Adara accepted the new name only because she believed that Katz was a Sephardic name of Greek origin.

The Upper West Side was a neighborhood a bit down on its luck, like much of New York. A mean kind of street crime, especially on the side streets, was driving people to the suburbs. Eighty-Sixth Street was a bit more appealing because it was safer, with less chance of being mugged or burgled. Still, there were always threats. It wasn't out of place for local radio to put out warnings about a man with a knife stabbing people on Amsterdam.

West Eighty-Sixth Street was wide and open and well-lit, though, and it didn't have the crime—nor the rats—that came with dark side streets. It was only crossed by wide avenues. The people who lived there didn't look like the people in their neighborhood in Queens. To Upper West Siders, Queens was just a place you passed through to get to the airport.

Things could get better. Art had often heard a promise: This part of Manhattan was a neighborhood "in transition." It was gaining the interest of real estate investors. Some residents were unhappy about that. Some didn't want their little shops and bakeries replaced by big, expensive chain stores.

But Art couldn't imagine anyone complaining about it. To him, a neighborhood "in transition" held the promise that it would someday be a place for rich people. Art could envision it now: There he was, with his family and their little restaurant in the neighborhood for wealthy Manhattanites. And they would not be driven out because, in Art's vision, he would buy their whole building. It was a small building in bad repair that their foolish landlord would probably be glad to unload.

Art could see it all. He believed in the transition the way their parents had believed in Saint Achilles, after whom he was named. Parents can teach their children unshakable faith but can't control where they direct it. It had been Art's idea to move to America, to New York, and it was only after they got there that Niki and Adara could see why. It was not the Statue of Liberty that inspired them. In fact, they never saw it. They arrived by plane at JFK airport and their first glimpse of the new land was the Belt Parkway. It wasn't until they saw Rockefeller Center with an enormous lit tree that Niki and Adara, too, started feeling that they had come to the right place. Yet it wasn't the tree or 30 Rockefeller Plaza that truly won them over but the people, the way they dressed, the way they skated like movie stars on perfectly maintained ice beneath towering buildings. To them, these were happy people with happy lives. It was the same feeling they used to get when they went over to the smiling island of Mykonos.

Besides, Art already seemed like a New Yorker. It suited him. Even the name Art suited him. It was soon difficult to remember that he had ever been called anything else. In their family, he was the brains. His brother Niki was the seducer. They were complete opposites. Niki's dark hair flowed in ringlets. He was one of a handful of Greek men born to every generation to prove that the ancient sculptors were not making it up. Art, though unmistakably Niki's brother, was the unseductive version. He did not have the smile or the eyes or the hair. In fact, his hair was thinning, a Grecian tragedy slowly unfolding. But he was savvy. When he first started renting on Eighty-Sixth Street, Art, wanting to appear to be a man of standing, took out a loan and bought a large black SUV with tinted windows. He could already imagine passersby wondering who he was.

This habit of the gods—of distributing charms and looks for one brother and brains for the other—is why it is often assumed that beautiful people are not smart. It was true in Niki's case, but his spellbindingly beautiful wife Adara was both. While most everyone else dismissed her as simply beautiful, Niki knew there was a deep intelligence underneath. In New York most people didn't appreciate it because it was a peasant kind of braininess. She understood a great deal more about goats than real estate, but Art, too, could see that she had a mind (although, to him, there was nothing more important than understanding real estate).

Once they opened the Katz Brothers, Niki greeted people because that was the only thing he was good at. He couldn't even make good cheese, but he was perfectly suited to welcome customers. Every restaurant should have a Niki—one Niki. Their diners thought he ran the restaurant. His smoldering brown eyes and broad, toothy smile softened everyone—even health inspectors. Talking to them was Niki's job, a special skill because they were accustomed to employees trying to seduce them. But the others weren't as good at it. Niki had what is sometimes termed "an almond butter smile." It was soft and delicious and seemed only one stage from melting. But his dark eyes didn't smile. They looked like they had seen the outer rings of Dante's hell. This look tends to be good for seduction because no one wants to feel that they're being seduced by a lightweight.

Adara and Niki also had a son, still a toddler, whom everyone insisted on calling Henry, though his real name was Hermes. He was fawned over because he had inherited the beauty genes of his parents, the perfect little Grecian god with dark curly hair and black eyes of polished lava.

Since the Katsikases were still proud cheesemakers, the food they served at the Katz Brothers centered on the various goat cheeses, both fresh and cured, that Adara made in Queens from the recipes of their island. She even made a "cheese cake," melopita, from fresh goat milk curds. The Katsikases had been pleased to discover that basic American diner food involved melting cheese on everything anyway. The customers didn't ask where the cheese came from, which helped avoid a number of burdensome city health regulations. Customers only knew that theirs was the best grilled cheese sandwich they had ever tasted. The mac and cheese, cheeseburger, and cheese omelets—complete with herbs that the Katsikases had grown in their backyard garden—were like no other.

Raising goats and making cheese in Queens was, as Art put it, "not exactly legal." This was New York. The city would not control rents but drew the line at goats—but who would know? Island people like the Katsikases know how to look after their own business. They bribed their neighbors with cheeses and fresh goat milk. The Milano family lived next door and, despite their name, were from Naples, but

Adara was certain they were really from Sicily. She was equally convinced that Sicilians were really Greek. Their original name must have been Milanos.

Joey and Anna Milano were not upset about goats next door. On the contrary, they were motivated by them. The Milanos made mozzarella in their dark, earth-scented basement from store-bought cow milk, but they had always wanted a water buffalo. Adara had once persuaded them to use her goat milk but they weren't happy with the result. They liked using it for ricotta, though. (Ricotta making, Adara informed Niki, proved that they were Sicilian and therefore Greek.) Their goat ricotta was just like her fresh cheese, myzithra, with which she made melopita. The Milanos made a beautiful cheesecake with theirs, with candied orange peel, dark chocolate chips, and orange blossom water.

For dessert at the Katz Brothers, Art had once considered serving Adara's melopita, but he didn't think it would appeal to their American customers. To have a foreign dessert that a diner clientele would have never heard of seemed too upscale. His mother's rice pudding recipe, he reasoned, would be far more appealing. (It was the only dish Art knew how to make: Art's "specialty.") He had also considered bringing in cheesecake from Grossinger's, the bakery on West Eighty-Eighth Street. Maybe the marble flavor. Or hazelnut? Art thought of pistachio. Their baker said they could do anything, but Art was hesitant about bringing in someone else's brand. Still, a New York cheesecake would be a good item for the diner. He would periodically talk to Herb Grosinger about possible arrangements. Should he credit Grossinger's, would it be a partnership? Art could never decide. Besides, Herb was in a constant fight with the landlords and Art was sure he would lose. He had already been driven out of his original shop farther down Columbus.

Art often thought of his "uncle," a close family friend who had become wealthy by setting up in Mykonos before the tourists came. That was what Art envisioned for himself on Eighty-Sixth Street. That was how to make money. Art thought it was ridiculous that there was a growing movement for New York City to control commercial rents, but Mayor Koch, leading the way into the 1980s, didn't back it anyway. Koch preferred the landlords who knew how to make wealth. To him, a neighborhood was built on its real estate development, not its cheesecake.

While the family was busy with the restaurant, the Milanos, who had two young children of their own, looked after "Henry." Adara hoped that when her son was old enough, she could bring him into the restaurant business. If she started him young he could have real meraki cooking, cooking with soul. That was what they called it at home—real feeling in his food, like she had. To have meraki meant to leave a piece of yourself in your work. Then Henry could learn all the tricks and grow up to be a great chef, the kind who never cooks but is always on television and makes a lot of money. For now, he was learning cheesemaking: goat cheese with Mom or mozzarella with the babysitters. Cheese is important too. Nothing wrong with meraki cheese. People taste the difference, though meraki cheeseburgers were not what Adara had in mind. And the Katz Brothers didn't yet have cheesecake.

2

The Real Place

By 1983, the Katz Brothers Greek diner had become a gathering place, especially for birds. If you looked up (which of course no one did because New Yorkers always look down, ignoring the local architecture to dodge unpleasant things on the sidewalk), you might notice a gathering of pigeons, like an Alfred Hitchcock movie scene, making their way to the corner of Eighty-Sixth Street and Columbus Avenue. Ruth Arnstein walked beneath them to the diner. As she went, Ruth would reach into her large white-and-orange Zabar's bag to pull out treats for the local dogs and $1 bills she dispensed to the needy. A substantial pigeon population, too—gray, brown, or white, thin or fat ones with rainbow oil-slick necks—gathered on the sidewalk to receive the stale bread morsels Ruth tossed out.

Ruth never noticed, but there was a constant rumbling from behind the tin-covered scaffolding of the neighboring building. It was a raccoon family oafishly stumbling over their long, sharp claws. It was fortunate that Ruth never heard them. If she'd known they were there, she would probably have tried to feed them, and that is a dangerous proposition. They look like cuddly tourists with sunglasses—but look again at their claws. Better to focus on pigeons.

The raccoons had moved to Eighty-Sixth Street from Central Park for the food. They quickly found garbage from the Katz Brothers, and the neighboring scaffolding provided a good shelter. The scaffolding should have come down by now, but the landlord, Abe Gonzalez, didn't pay his bills, so the city-mandated work was not getting done. He owned but had not paid taxes on the Katz Brothers' building, either, and Art heard that he had gotten into trouble with the city. The apartments above the Katz Brothers were known to be a good place to live in the neighborhood, but units were never available. The old-time tenants seldom moved. Although Gonzalez hadn't maintained the property very well, he also didn't try to raise rents or evict tenants who often didn't pay.

No one was fooled into thinking Gonzalez was good-hearted. It was clear that he was just lazy. Art had long dreamed of buying him out, since he could see Gonzalez didn't have the brains of the landlord who threw out Grossinger's. He dreamed of raising the rents, driving all the tenants out, and fixing up the building for "a classier clientele." The neighborhood started to see Art's point of view when it became known that Gonzalez's buildings were infested with bedbugs. A young beagle named Max was sent in to sniff every corner and crevice to find them. Then an elaborate treatment had to be performed on all the furniture, paintings, possessions. The bedbugs seemed to travel from one apartment to another, and the neighbors worried that they would spread to other buildings. Even after it became clear that tenants on the rest of the block were safe, many hired Max to sniff their apartments at their landlords' expense because they wanted to see him in action. Mimi Landau, who had as crammed an apartment as anyone in the neighborhood, loved watching Max work for hours. There were no bedbugs. Good work, Max.

Niki, not one to care about property value, nonetheless dreamed of getting rid of the raccoons. A gentle, pleasant man with no temper, he had this one failing. He hated raccoons. He was afraid of them. Not a man of violence, he walked up to Ronald, the tall, pleasant, well-dressed man who stood quietly across the street from the synagogue on Saturday morning with a wire coming out of his ear into his suit.

"Excuse me."

Ronald smiled but kept looking across the street.

"Do you have a gun?"

Ronald stopped smiling.

"No, no," said Niki. "It's just that there are raccoons in the neighborhood."

This did not produce the expected reaction. Ronald smiled and said, "I know. I've seen them."

"Do you think you can shoot them?"

"No sir, it's illegal to harm them. They are protected by the government."

Even worse, he told Niki that the government had a program to give raccoons vaccinations so that they would stay healthy.

"Some neighborhood you picked," Niki later said to his brother, with whom he was never angry. Art, who had picked the neighborhood without knowing about the raccoons, had no answer.

. . .

Art had installed in the diner a chrome-edged Formica counter with chrome-and-green leather-seated stools in a row in front of it. There were a few chrome-edged tables that more or less matched the counter, which people used when the counter was all taken. The linoleum floor was easy to clean, and with its splotchy pattern it would never reveal it if it wasn't.

Inside, eating a grilled cheese sandwich and drinking a Diet Pepsi for lunch, was Violette de Lussac. She didn't know about the raccoons and had her sandwich and Pepsi as often as she needed it. Understanding that her life, along with her name, was entirely detached from reality, she found lunch at the Greek diner to be a return to that old world she'd lived in when she had a real name. She would sit at table or on one of the green leather counter stools in her designer dress, with bracelets and earrings that looked as though they'd been created by a famous sculptor. Sometimes she would wear a simple shift, but that was because she had learned how to wear one so that it would show off her body.

Violette was one of numerous loyal neighborhood customers. Lazarus Vanderthal frequented the place, too. It was assumed that his was a made-up name, but unlike Violette and Art Katz, Lazarus used the name with which he'd been born. A young man with a sloppy kind of intensity, Lazarus took dates there because it was the only restaurant in the neighborhood where he could afford a meal for two. He

would extravagantly suggest Caesar salad with good anchovies and even a little goat cheese that he claimed had been
made by the Katz brothers themselves. His dates were generally irritated by his choice of restaurant and didn't want a
salad for dinner. He seldom brought the same woman twice.
Once, while he was walking a date home, the pair encountered two raccoons looking like the Blues Brothers. This did
not help his cause.

Lazarus, despite having an aristocratic-sounding name, was
a neighborhood kid. When he was eleven years old, his father
died of a heart attack while operating the Broadway Local 1
train. This showed Lazarus, and probably many of the people
on the train, that fate was not something that could be predicted. A great deal of attention was given to the accident.
There was not much interest in the fact that his father really
did die. Apparently more importantly, three passengers had
as well. It was implied that the driver escaped prosecution by
dying too. His mother had served lunches at P.S. 84 on West
Ninety-Second Street and lived in the neighborhood in a
small rent-controlled one-bedroom. She would often pick up
a black-and-white cookie from Grossinger's on the way home
as a treat for young Lazarus, his introduction to Hungarian
baking.

Linda was often there, which was about all that could be
said about her. No one knew her last name. If a person only
goes by one name, surely it should be something better than
Linda. She would get a table and turn to various customers
and ask questions that she may have thought were thought-
provoking, but that had an opposite effect. There was no
way to answer such questions as "Are rare cheeseburgers
safe?" or "Can bedbugs enter through an open window?"

No one did answer Linda. When she got the rare answer, everyone could see that the responder was not from the neighborhood.

Albert Hoffman, A. G. Hoffman, was once a metro reporter for the *New York Times* who had covered some now-forgotten controversies and then profiled artists and musicians for the arts section, had a brief stint in science, and eventually was writing obituaries. But his passion had been limericks. He wrote limericks for every obit but, of course, never showed them to anyone.

> There was a producer named Strauss
> Who everyone knew was a louse . . .

These limericks were his secret that he kept in a notebook, where he also saved words that he hoped to one day rhyme. Hypoxia, the lack of oxygen he often felt in the world; vermillion. Shemozzle (he had already used kerfuffle) was a word he'd hoped to use some day. Writing the life stories of people more interesting than he was had proven depressing, so he had retired, taken a buyout with enough money to live on. He came into the Katz Brothers every day at twelve thirty and ordered a tuna on rye with extra mayonnaise and an iced tea. He put a great deal of sugar in his iced tea—that was all anyone knew about him.

On Wednesdays at three, the Haitian artist Ti Auguste would come in with two friends. They'd previously met at a little Haitian café that served lambi and dangerous sauce ti-malice and stocked the latest Creole language newspapers, but it had closed almost ten years earlier. Now, as far as these three knew, they were the last holdouts in this once Haitian neighborhood. As they sauntered in, Niki greeted them and shook hands with each of them. They sat at a four-top.

"Frites?" offered Niki.

"Mais oui," the three answered, the two syllables scaling down an octave.

The restaurant always smelled of French fries even after it closed for the evening. This may have appealed to raccoons, but fries were also one of the popular items with customers. The oil was always hot to make the fries crisp. Niki set down a large platter that the three picked at while arguing in Haitian Creole. Their voices would vigorously ascend to high notes before furiously descending again, sometimes as they waved or limply pointed a French fry for emphasis. Even Niki, who understood French, had no idea what the three were arguing about. After two hours they would pay the bill, smack their hands together as though washing off the argument, and leave. Until the next Wednesday.

Art knew these customers would not be here forever. Several other inexpensive restaurants like the Cherry Restaurant, once next to Grossinger's, had already been driven off. Grossinger's would not be far behind. Art could see that the Katz Brothers would not last much longer either. It had been surviving the lively eighties but would not be fit for the nineties. Customers might have seen it too, because they often made suggestions for how the diner could get more business. Saul Putz (pronounced *pootz*, he quickly added when he gave out his business card, which he did with the persistence of an oak tree offering acorns) had some ideas.

Another Katz Brothers regular, Saul was the producer of the most popular food show on television and thus supposed he knew what was trendy and what would sell. He tried to convince Art to turn the shop into a kosher restaurant, which would be popular with attendees of the Modern Orthodox synagogue down the street. He argued that several kosher restaurants had popped up in the neighborhood and they all charged high prices and did well. But Art thought the Katsikases had pushed their Jewishness as far as they could.

In truth, Saul could understand a certain hesitation about becoming a kosher restaurant. He himself avoided them. He came to the Katz Brothers because no one from his Orthodox group would ever set foot in there and catch him eating his BLT. Okay, forget the kosher restaurant. Saul didn't even send his daughter, Masha, to the Orthodox synagogue. Another idea: Putz suggested they add more menu options for kids after school. Heeding the call, the Katz Brothers added a special on platters of fries and an ice cream freezer with six flavors, three normal and three weird: strawberry shortcake, bubble gum, and goat cheese with cherries and nettles.

To Art's surprise, once ice cream was available, the hightoned Violette suggested they add root beer floats. She said she'd grown up on them and loved them. Art didn't know if he should believe her but he thought the floats might be a good conversation starter with her. He started offering them and she started ordering them, but still she conversed little with Art. The new ice cream menu made the diner hugely popular at four in the afternoon. With most of the bakeries gone, where else was there to go? Masha came in with her parents. She would always order a vanilla malted. Only after being told that they couldn't make one would she order a root beer float like everyone else.

As though to one-up a root beer float, another regular named Serafina suggested that they serve egg creams, which was something the Katsikases had never heard of because they were not Katzes. Since she wanted egg creams, Serafina may not have really been a Serafina either. She was always dressed in brightly colored, well-fitting, unusual outfits with great floppy hats. A working girl, she had stood on Columbus Avenue before it was cleaned up and she, the bakeries, and the antique shops were forced out. She lived in a studio apartment in Violette's building. When it went co-op she had refused to buy in and was now the only rental tenant left. She found customers through more subtle means now, sometimes at the Katz Brothers. A. G. Hoffman had met her there and ended up calling her number on a lonely night. Ever after, he was paralyzed with embarrassment when he saw her on the street.

Serafina thought her friend Mimi, another long-established Upper West Sider who always had unusual friends, would come to the diner if they served egg creams. But Mimi knew that the Katsikas brothers were interested in buildings like hers and, early on, recognized that they were the enemy. In any event, the egg creams didn't work. Serafina showed Art how to freeze the milk and shoot in the seltzer, but the soft-drink dispenser didn't have enough force.

. . .

Even as he made these little changes to keep customers happy, Art had known what he was ultimately going to do with the neighborhood. It had just been a question of timing. When Gonzalez was finally forced to put their building up for sale after defaulting on his property taxes, Art pounced. The early eighties had been the time to prepare for their second assimilation. He could tell some people and not others about his plan. In a couple years, the Upper West Side was going to become an "upscale neighborhood," he told Violette, happy to have another excuse to talk to her. He promised fine stores and apartments. But Art could see that somehow news of the coming changes saddened Violette. She stared at the Formica as she noisily sucked on her root beer float. Art wondered what he had said that was wrong.

3

Coming of Age

Violette de Lussac was the sum of her parts, even before she was Violette de Lussac. Though men didn't always agree on which part they liked best, they always pursued her. Some older men said they liked her for her legs. Some even admired her feet, which had long toes. Men with no imagination were in pursuit of her plump posterior, and the least inventive of all admired her breasts. There was little to be gained by knowing the men who pursued her. As Proust said, "Let us leave pretty women to men with no imagination." But what does that leave pretty women with?

Originally, she was pursued without a poetic name. She was born at the end of the Depression. Veronika Patowski. "Patowski" came from one of those Catholic southern New England towns where, aside from a few Italians, most everyone was either Irish or Polish. "Veronika" was a bit of each, which was not unusual.

The town, on the outskirts of the industrial end of Hartford, was a leading producer of nameless doohickeys, prosaic industrial contraptions that were used in larger factories to produce more recognizable things such as lawn mowers, air conditioners, and helicopters. The largest factory in town made ball bearings. When Veronika left the small town, she was shocked to learn that there are quite a few people in the world who don't even know that a ball bearing is a smooth steel ball, a few of which, in the right places, help a machine move more smoothly. Understanding ball bearings was what separated a local from an out-of-towner. As a young teenager, Veronika imagined that she operated with ball bearings in her hips. The eighth-grade science teacher, Mr. Ronkowski, said that hips did have ball bearings called bursa.

In the early 1950s, when Veronika was just fourteen, her Irish mother crashed her car into a tree and died. In retellings, it was always implied that alcohol was involved, but that was only part of the story. Her mother had become dizzy from medication she was taking for an allergic reaction to a bug bite. Veronika never learned why her mother crashed into the tree—or why she named her Veronika, why it was with a K instead of a C—or anything else about her. Her father, a foreman in a factory that made a part of a machine that manufactured ball bearings, did what all parents in this town did with children they did not know what else to do with, children who asked too many questions, girls whom boys liked too much. He sent Veronika to a nearby Catholic boarding school where, at bargain prices, she could be beaten by unknowable women in black robes.

One day Veronika peeked into a humid room where Sister Mary—one of several Sister Marys, but the nice one, who always smelled like Dial soap—was undressing to take a shower. This was a rare opportunity: There was great speculation among the girls about what the sisters wore under their habits. The first surprise came when Sister Mary unwrapped her elaborate headgear. Veronika had always heard rumors that the nuns shaved their heads, but Sister Mary unpinned thick auburn hair that rolled over her shoulders like a bolt of satin. She removed her robe and then proceeded to undo an array of strange cotton contraptions—some laced, some buttoned, nothing so banal as to use a zipper.

When she was at last naked, it was an astonishing sight. Veronika, already quite proud of her own parts, saw that Sister Mary outdid her—her large, soft, pink breasts, an ass which, to Veronika's fury, seemed even better than her own. Sister Mary was keeping hidden a sublime work. No one would know that Veronika had been outdone by a nun. No one would know. That was the good thing about voluptuous nuns. Although she was not particularly devout, it had not occurred to Veronika to doubt the existence of God. Sister Mary's body was his magnificent gift. Yet God would not have created such greatness unless he intended for people to see it, to appreciate it. It was a sin to hide it. Bodies were made to be seen. Otherwise, why have them?

This became Veronika's only religious conviction. At least she had one. Catholic school had not been a waste. Here she was, age fourteen and perfect. Maybe not as perfect as Sister Mary, but no one was ever going to know that. Veronika was pleased to have recently developed not only hair between her legs but a light dusting of reddish strands under her arms that she was too proud of to shave. They weren't supposed to shave anyway. The school didn't give them razors. It was bad enough that they had periods, also frowned upon by the sisters. Not as bad as not having one.

It was not right that she should remain hidden and unseen under her gray flannel uniform. Soon she would be almost the age the men in her town had thought she was. She longed to bare herself—to someone. It wasn't going to be at school. So she took her body and left. She ran away to New York.

. . .

A late night and a long bus ride to New York later, she got a room at the Hotel Earle for four dollars a night. No one asked her age. She didn't know exactly what she was going to do. The dark but clean building—she thought it was clean, too dark to be sure—seemed full of people in the exact same dilemma. People seemed to come to New York to wait for something to happen. Many of them waited in the lobby.

Maybe she should try to meet one of them here. She thought her body was all the introduction she would need. Had she been a pretty girl—even a very pretty girl—her age would have been obvious. But in her eyes, she already had a womanly beauty that obscured her age.

Wandering out, she bought a copy of the *Village Voice* and sat in a café and ordered a glass of red wine. She didn't really want it but she wanted to see if she could pass for eighteen. The wine was served by a waitress who cared no more about Veronika's age than Veronika did about hers. The waitress had a tattoo on her shoulder the likes of which Veronika had never seen. As a matter of fact, she had never seen a woman with a tattoo—only men with anchors. Her uncle had been in the Navy and had an anchor on his chest. But he'd had a heart attack, and after open-heart surgery the two sides of the anchor hadn't aligned. This had worked out in her favor: He didn't want to go shirtless in front of her anymore.

This waitress had a flower on her shoulder, which made much more sense. It could even survive heart surgery. If you're going to show your body you might as well decorate it somehow, Veronika thought. The flower on the waitress was a daisy. The waitress was named Daisy, evident from the name tag pinned on her blouse. Veronika thought that Daisy was not much of a name, nor much of a flower, for an exotic tattooed Greenwich Village waitress. Couldn't she have picked a better flower? She could have had a violet, been a Violette, Veronika thought as she sipped her red wine, which, by the way, was really sour and unpleasant. She paid the bill and then, after reflecting on the first tip she had ever left, threw in an extra quarter for Daisy. And that was how fourteen-year-old Veronika entered a Greenwich Village café and emerged as eighteen-year-old Violette.

She next went into a small, dark Italian café with a huge ornate metal machine that was making tiny cups of something black. The drink looked like the one made by the Italian men who used to live in her town, yet she had never tasted it. They had called it a "demitasse." She ordered one, though the waiter looked at her oddly when she said "demitasse." He brought it anyway.

It was the most bitter drink she had ever tasted. She was experiencing everything. There had been sour and now there was bitter. The café also served a decorated cheesecake wrapped in green marzipan. She recognized this cheesecake from the Italian bakery in her hometown, which had decorated theirs with flowers made of candied pumpkin. It was so sweet that it grabbed at your throat. But Veronika had already experienced the cake, so Violette didn't order it. Instead, she sipped the demitasse as the bitterness seized the cells of her tongue, crept across her mouth, tightened her nerves. She could only endure one small sip at a time, but soon those tiny sips became extraordinary. Espresso tasted so much like what she hoped life would be: lively and intense. She had not yet experienced that kind of life, but when she did she knew she would sip it slowly.

The man at the newsstand who sold her the *Village Voice* had said that the ads were the best part of the paper. She started looking through them, sipping. There were boats to rent, including a Chinese junk; positions available for jugglers; requests for tattoo artists; one ad for a seal trainer; and a whole column of ads for artist's models.

Artist's model.

Did other lives have such moments? Did Darwin see an ad for biologists or Rembrandt for painters? Did Edison see an ad for lightbulb builders wanted? Maybe her town had been founded by someone who saw an ad that said "ball bearing makers wanted." Was that how these things happened?

When Violette saw those words, "artist's model," she instantly realized it was what she had been meant to do. This was what God had meant for her. She didn't know which ad to pick, so she chose the second one simply because it wasn't the first. It could have been a bad choice. She called the number and made an appointment with a man with a bored tone of voice, a man who sounded like he wanted to be thinking about something else. Also, the apartment wasn't in Greenwich Village where artists lived. It was way up in some depressing neighborhood on West Eighty-Sixth Street. This was not an artist's address. It seemed to her that it was the address of someone who wanted to become one, perhaps a pervert who just wanted to look at naked women—though she wasn't certain that would qualify him as a pervert.

She studied a map posted on the corner of West Fourth Street and Sixth Avenue and took the C train. She hadn't taken the subway before. It was loud and crowded and a gray-haired man in a suit was deliberately rubbing the back of his hand against her. He got off at Forty-Second Street, but by Seventy-Second a bald man had replaced him. Violette thought the man she was meeting was probably, at least, better than the men on the C train. After all, a man who placed ads in the *Village Voice* for women to come to his apartment and take off their clothes was certainly far ahead of a man who goes groping in the subway.

Columbus Avenue was rough and dirty—sidewalks piled with garbage, scraps blowing in the wind, broken bottles and flattened cigarette butts, crumbling brownstones and decrepit brick buildings. Even some of the people looked unhealthy. It looked like the kind of street her father had told her to avoid, but when she got to West Eighty-Sixth Street it looked surprisingly presentable, with large buildings displaying green-awning entrances guarded by men in uniforms. She had been right—this was not a neighborhood for artists.

She walked too far west in an effort to distance herself from Columbus and had to turn back to find the awning with the right building number. She was greeted by a man in uniform. He looked like one of the volunteer firemen in her hometown who wore military-type uniforms of their own design for the Fourth of July parade. As instructed, she entered the elevator and pushed the button marked PH, although she doubted that a real artist would live in a penthouse. She vaguely recalled that PH had something to do with her chemistry class.

When she stepped out she was in someone's apartment. A tall, lean man was waiting for her. She was generally not fond of lean bodies, but this one she thought was all right. Inviting her in, he introduced himself as Guy Witman, said as though the name had some meaning. Maybe, Violette thought, he was like her, trying out a new name for the first time. Guy had long straight hair that flopped over his face, affording him the opportunity to periodically jerk his head and flip it back. He wore a puffy linen shirt. She could see his tricks. That hair was beyond just needing a haircut and the shirt was not just a size too large. For a linen shirt to puff just right you had to have a lean, perfectly fit body.

The job was hers if she wanted it. She knew this because he was looking at her the way the plump women back home looked into the window of Angela's Pastry Shop at the green marzipan cheesecakes.

She introduced herself. "Violette de Lussac." It just popped out. She didn't even know where the "de Lussac" part came from, and she worried she might be going a little too far. Maybe it was because she had been thinking about those candied decorations. But she could tell that he accepted the name without question. Who could believe a name like that? Veronika had once asked Sister Mary, "Don't you ever doubt the teachings?" Sister Mary replied, "No. I am blessed with the gift of belief." This irritated Veronika, who wanted to answer back, "Yeah, and the gift of a big butt," but held her tongue because the Sisters were armed with rulers that really hurt. Guy, too, clearly had the gift of belief, so when he asked Violette how old she was, she was surprised to hear herself answer, "Twenty-three."

"Oh, I'm twenty-five," he answered pleasantly, yanking his head to toss his hair from his face. He definitely had the gift. Violette's life changed in that moment. But it took years for her to understand the price. It was 1952, the year Eisenhower was elected and Jackson Pollock first exhibited his "drip" paintings, a year of contrasts. That was the instant her teenage years were erased. She became subdued, trying to act mature, sipping, always sipping.

Guy's was a daylight-drenched apartment with tall windows—a silvery polished moonlit place on the right nights. It is not well known that there is no full moon more brazen than the one that shines over the Upper West Side on a clear night. Astronomers, or at least stargazers, should use the term "Upper West Side moon." Like a ripe fruit, it glows so high above that it makes you realize the skyscrapers barely scrape the sky. Beyond the windows was a large terrace, and beyond that was the majesty of Manhattan, its staggered buildings rising to competing heights. With an excitement that she was trying to suppress—excitement was a certain youthful giveaway—she identified the ornate metallic needle of the Empire State Building.

The apartment was cluttered with painted canvases of all sizes hung on walls and stacked on floors. There was something appealing about his paintings, the extravagant brush-strokes, the true and honest colors, the way he comfortably glided between figurative and abstract, as though he were redefining reality. She later learned that quite a number of people had thought this before.

. . .

Even when she was fully dressed, he could see her so completely that it almost didn't matter when she peeled off her clothes, really pointless obstructions. Her only awkwardness came because she didn't have nice underwear, so she slid out of them as quickly as possible. Once she was naked, she felt proud. Guy positioned her on a large cushion, curled her legs and only slightly spread them. Her arms were placed above her head. He told her not to move and began sketching. He worked for hours. This was harder work than she had imagined. She wanted to be good at this so she did not move. Occasionally he would spray her skin to make her a little shiny, like one might do for a car or a pair of shoes. She was an object. She was surprised to find that being an object was harder work than being a person. She didn't mind. She recalled a phrase she had learned somewhere, "objet d'art." That was what she was becoming, an art object. The thought made her smile.

"No. No," he said. "Don't smile."

Guy Witman could look at most anything and only see what was alive and what was beautiful. Like the poet Rilke once said of the sculptor Rodin, "His art was not based on a great idea, but upon the conscious realization of something small." He wanted to communicate the beauty that he saw. While his painting was not painstaking realism, he did not miss the details—the curve of her neck, the orange fleece under her arms, the way her toes did not curl. He saw it all.

When he was finished and the sunlight was fading, reddening low in the sky over New Jersey, Guy shed his own clothes, walked naked onto the terrace, and climbed into a hot tub surrounded by leafy plants. He invited her to join him but she put her clothes on and left. She wanted modeling to be her profession.

Once he started paying her, the first thing she bought was better underwear. Lingerie. She usually worked in the afternoon light and never joined Guy in the hot tub at dusk. Then he asked her to start posing at night. She wondered whether this had another meaning, but it was soon apparent to her that it only meant a different kind of light. The big ripe moon had a phosphorescence as blue as the heart of a flame. The objects it lit seemed to capture it and throw it back. After all, the moon had no light of its own either. All this reflected light was so bright she could barely make out the face of the man smiling down at her. (The artist, that is, not the moon.) He seemed to know that this painting was her destiny, maybe because it was his, too.

After many nights at work on the painting, he put down his brush. It was like marrying a knife and fork when the meal is done. For the first time she looked at the canvas. She was beautiful in pale blue light. Broad strokes defined the curves of her body, and even with few features, he had captured her face. *How could a painting so abstract be so sexy?* she wondered. She only knew that his vision of her was more beautiful than she could ever be. It came from him, she thought, not from her.

Her job was done. That night she bathed with him in the hot tub, draped in steam in the blue moonlight. From the first kiss, everything was the way she had always imagined it would be—gentle and exciting. He handled her, part by part, like caressing sacred objects. He was an artist.

Later in the night, she lay across his bed resting and thought, *Now it is sealed.* Some lies dissolve like ice cream melting on hot apple pie. After a while its shape is gone. She knew that her lie was not one of them. It must never be seen. He could never know her real age—ever.

. . .

The art world, which decides these things, decided that *Violette in Moonlight* was a masterpiece of post-modernism, a work of genius, a new chapter in twentieth-century art. (It was also very sexy, but no one would say that, which was a good thing. Sex always ended up being criticized later.) A small, respected French magazine called Guy "a master of eroticism." He was a master of eroticism in some New York circles too, but it made him nervous. America had moralists, ready to attack. He was already well known in Paris from a show at Studio Paul Facchetti, the same gallery that had first showcased Pollock. He'd also had an important show at the Whitney. But now he was amassing pieces for the most important show in his still-young career, this time at the Museum of Modern Art. He did a few more paintings of Violette and some landscapes and even a few still lifes.

Of course, those of Violette sold for the highest prices. A Witman Violette was now worth something. Several major museums acquired them. The original moonlight went to the Tate in London, which outbid the Paris Museum of Modern Art, and soon private collectors were paying six and seven figures for them. Whenever Guy wanted money, he could sell a Violette. He bought a small farm outside the city with a single piece.

Everything sold. As a joke he did a still life of violets, and even that sold for six figures to a wealthy German who did not even get the joke. And Violette herself? She was like a live, walking, talking Mona Lisa. She became the most sought-after model in the art world. She sat for many leading New York and New England artists. A Spanish artist flew her to Barcelona to pose for him. She was commissioned to model for a sculptor in Berlin.

Violette took her career, and also herself, seriously and refused to sleep with any of her clients. This at times was a disappointment to the artists, but it increased demand for her as a model. She married Guy, the believer, and they lived together in his penthouse high above the West Side. This made her name Violette de Lussac Witman, but that didn't matter. She was known to everyone, even the doormen, simply as Violette.

The uncomfortable subject of age rarely came up. When she was forty-three, at the age of thirty-four, she had a "miracle baby." Guy painted a nude of her seven months pregnant that sold for one of his highest prices yet, partly because he had wanted to keep it, forcing the buyer to offer more. The baby was a girl, Jasmine. Through diet and exercise Violette maintained her famous body and, in her fifties, looked like she was only in her forties (which she was). Guy didn't paint Jasmine because he didn't want to make her a part of what he thought was a silly narrative that art writers had created about their family.

Jasmine misunderstood and thought her father refused to paint her because she was not beautiful enough. Luck once again having its own way, Jasmine did not inherit her mother's body. But also she fed her bitterness with large amounts of food—Homeric quantities of ice cream sandwiches and a difficult-to-explain passion for Tootsie Rolls. She had been a pudgy baby, a chubby little girl.

In her teenage years, desperate to make sense of her situation, she found a psychology book that provided her with what everyone wants: a reason to blame their parents. She learned that women who deferred childbearing until their forties often have children with many problems. One of the problems listed was obesity. When Jasmine confronted her mother, Violette had no defense, no usable argument. Jasmine was angry and she remained angry. It was as though being fat was at once her great punishment and great revenge, and it was effective. Once she left school, in her final act of vengeance, she launched her career in an insurance company.

As a girl, Violette had come from people who longed to wear suits, turn their backs on good union benefits to leave factories and work in insurance. The women in insurance wore suits just like the men. Too bad, thought Violette, that the men didn't have better taste to imitate. For Violette the only thing worse than going into insurance would have been working at a ball bearing factory. Jasmine might have done that, but she didn't know that part of her mother's history—thank God. Hadn't Violette spared Jasmine that path?

So Jasmine parlayed a natural ability with mathematics (where did that come from?) into a high-paying job as an actuary. By analyzing health and lifestyle statistics she could predict clients' likelihood of an accident or even death. Of course, she could never have made accurate predictions about her mother because the data was completely off, but no one knew that.

Age was not a usual subject in Violette's home. It did arise with Matsunosake, a landscape designer Guy had commissioned to redesign their terrace with a spectacular garden. He had built Japanese gardens in public and private spaces throughout New York, Long Island, and New England, and a few in California. Like Violette, he had a last name that no one used.

Matsu told Violette that a garden always had to have "aware," a Japanese word he carefully pronounced in three syllables. It meant a sense of the passage of time—not a favorite idea for Violette—embracing the cycles of nature, of life and death. To him, a garden was not so much a reflection of nature as an exaggeration of it, and an expression of its owner. This garden, he said, should say "Violette." Matsu promised that it would have colors designed to be seen in the moonlight.

According to him, the spiritual center of the garden was the stone lantern he installed, though it was not entirely traditional. It had the usual kurin, the dome-like top; but then the kasa, the cap, was flat and protruded from the base on all sides like a cantilevered Frank Lloyd Wright house. The windows in the "light chamber" were modernist triangles.

Matsu, Violette thought, had a poetic soul that was extremely sexy. But he was also kind. He brought Jasmine a Japanese cheesecake which he called fuwa-fuwa. He said this one was much lighter and had far fewer calories than the traditional kind. Jasmine was offended.

Matsu planted sazanka, a camellia with large white blossoms whose perfume dominated the terrace, and small trees, kasha, and a kind of dwarf oak, dripping with rare white and purple orchids—a hearty breed that could withstand New York's reasonably mild winters. He planted fragrant leaves, too: burdock, kale, mustard, and deep beds of green-leafed, purple-veined amaranth. For color, he planted mauve-colored ageratum and red valerian growing up the wall by the apartment window and evergreen berberis with its hanging yellow cups and abelia triflora with sweet-smelling pink flowers that bloomed in the fall.

The terrace had good southern exposure for sunlight from both sides, so the plants flourished as the butterflies came in spring and summer and even fall to sip from blossoms. The garden twinkled with large white, blue, and orange commas and pipevine swallowtails with bright red spots like jewels on their black wings. Orange sulphurs, a brilliant yellow as though they had their own sunlight, liked to perch on the red valerian by the window where Guy painted and became a favorite subject. Butterflies liked Guy and would perch on him, and he'd often offer them his left hand so he could paint them with his right. Butterflies do not perch on everyone. They have their favorites.

The butterflies would not perch on Violette or Matsu or any of the art critics who came through the apartment to admire the garden. Violette was surprised that they would not perch on Matsu despite his closeness to nature, his sense of aware, his poetic soul. Maybe butterflies saw things differently. Violette wondered if they only liked people with the gift of belief.

Matsu was pleased that they already had a hot tub on the terrace. He said it could be the garden's tsukubai, their teahouse pond, or a passable substitute. But he did not like the tub's squareness. Right angles were unnatural. Over time, he brought in a variety of rocks, showing up with them one at a time, caressing each unique form, managing their weight with his sinewy limbs, placing them around and in the tub until it looked like an irregularly shaped pond. Some were angular, some round, some seemed like abstract sculptures. To him they all were sculptures. He had to be extremely strong—Violette could not lift these rocks that he casually jaunted in holding. He seemed to know exactly where each belonged.

He erected a stone bridge above the tub, too—an impressive though small feat of engineering. The true exhibitionists in her crowd—she was one of them—could prance naked on it while others in the hot tub gazed through the steam at their bobbing parts. It became a rite in their circle. Most anyone who was anyone had displayed themselves naked in Violette's garden. They did not have to be beautiful. In art, standard beauty could be a false value. Artists and critics and curators would crawl like reptiles out of the hot tub and sun themselves, sprawled in the amaranth or the thick grove of red siam, simmering like undercooked roasts in herbal marinade.

So Violette knew quite a lot about the people in New York art. She knew of the museum director with flabby sides, and the curator with saggy breasts but luscious thighs, and the painter with a long penis. A long penis is the original "elephant in the room." Everyone sees it and no one comments.

There were no higher buildings around, giving them considerable privacy except from helicopters that often passed over. And there could've been onlookers with binoculars farther downtown: midtown voyeurs. Violette hoped so. She loved the idea of affluent, proper people in high midtown apartments, maybe penthouses too, spying on her nakedness.

Actually, unknown to Guy and Violette, on the thirty-third floor of a new building on West Sixty-Eighth Street lived Lawrence Hemspan, owner of a small marketing firm and also of a telescope. He spent hours examining Violette's garden while pretending to be stargazing. He "loved astronomy," and not even his wife knew anything different.

. . .

Each time Matsu came by, he would lead Violette by the hand and show her what he was working on in the garden. If Guy was away, Matsu and Violette would make love in the garden right where Lawrence Hemspan could watch. The possibility of onlookers only added to the excitement.

Guy never worried about the attention Matsu gave to his wife. He trusted her. He was a believer. But Matsu was different than the worshipful Guy. Matsu was feral and took her hungrily, lifting her, turning her, doing what he wanted with his incredibly powerful limbs. She knew that for him part of the adventure was having an older woman, which was disturbing because in reality she was barely older than he was. For all his animal ferocity, he knew she liked him for his poetic nature. He seduced her with it as they lay flushed by the red-striped sunset of New Jersey, Manhattan turning to a dark eighteen-karat gold as he spoke again of his three-syllabled aware. As they lay in the warm light like prawns in melted butter, he spoke of "mono no aware," how beautiful sunsets made him enjoy the passing of life. "Mono no aware." Watching the sun set, she realized this was why she didn't feel so guilty. Time was passing. Matsu was only the second man she had ever had and, after all, shouldn't everyone have had at least two lovers? And how fortunate she was to have one with an artist's soul and one with a poet's. Afterward Matsu would pluck a rare sky-blue chrysanthemum and slowly brew it in an earthen pot as they shared the hot tub and he spoke of his life's sadness.

. . .

Guy liked to wake up early and paint by his window amid the morning light and birdsongs. Why do birds sing more in the morning than in the evening? The birds visited from Central Park only two blocks away: soprano warblers chirping, throaty doves cooing, the timpani of iridescent black grackles croaking. Guy liked the way the grackles jumped into the air before they spread their wings instead of other birds that do it the other way around—a leap of faith in the truest sense. Grackles too had the gift of belief. Flickers sang and thrashers whistled and sparrows sang counterpoint. Guy's morning painting was accompanied by a feathered cantata.

Violette liked the chubby, black-throated blue warbler with the fine flat head, though it was not really chubby or flatheaded. That was just how it wore its feathers, like the silhouette of a woman's dress concealing her body. Guy said that it was the perfect bird for her and wanted to paint her with one perched on her. But unlike Violette, the warbler would not sit still long enough to be painted. Modeling is not for everybody.

There was only one bird that Violette did not like: a large red-tailed hawk that nested in the masonry off to the side of the garden. Such a bird was unusual enough in New York for several ornithologists to have come to see it. They said it was a female and that a larger, deeper-colored male was probably "around somewhere." Violette, who formed opinions easily, didn't like the hawk's face, the brilliant yellow eyes staring forward as though they could see through her. The curved beak between the eyes looked dangerous, although Violette was informed that it was the talons that were the real weapons, not the beak. This was a predator, a hunter, a killer. It looked like the art critic Naomi Greenfield—same eyes, same beak. She feared the hawk would eat the warblers and sparrows and all the birds she loved. But the ornithologists assured her that she was wrong, that the hawk would not eat the other birds. The hawks had come to perch high over West Eighty-Fifth Street, waiting to feed on the rats from the sidewalk below. This in no way made her happier about the hawk.

. . .

Guy was now into what would later be called his "Roman period." The figures he painted were pale and marble-like. There were Doric elements to the sky, patterns in the blue. The canvases looked stark. Some critics raved about them. A few attacked them. Some had never wanted him to move on from *Violette in Moonlight*. But it was too late. Guy was reading Romans: the amusing little poems of Martial; Cato on farming; Virgil's epic of a warrior fleeing to Rome, which he found somehow depressing, though he thought he wasn't supposed to. He read Seneca's "On the Shortness of Life," which was really about making life feel longer. He often switched to the Greeks to quote Hippocrates: "Life is short, art is long." Good words for a seventy-two-year-old painter.

Age had once again become an issue, not because of the Roman classics but because of the *New York Times* arts section, which published an article headlined "Violette at 70." This had been Violette's fear for many years: that the lie would become unlivable. After the *Times* piece it seemed everyone wanted to write about Violette at seventy, which wasn't something Violette at sixty-one wanted to talk about. She sent away reporters and refused to pose for the photographers eager to show how great she looked for her age. But only two years earlier, she had posed nude for Larry Godard, a photographer of some note and considerable grace. It hadn't seemed like a bad idea to Violette at the time, but now those photographs were being printed as though they showed a crossroad of history. And it was a crossroad, really. Biology meets mathematics. Wasn't she remarkable? Didn't she look great? Was there anyone she could slap?

She wanted to tell the truth to someone, but she couldn't— especially not with Naomi the hawk out hunting. Naomi had pursued a campaign to stop exhibitions of the work of Paul Gauguin because her research had revealed that the artist had been debauching some of the underaged half-naked Tahitian girls he had once painted. *What research?* sneered Violette. Like Guy, part of Gauguin's appeal, though no one wanted to admit it, was eroticism. Anyone who looked at those paintings could see his life in Tahiti and why he preferred it to France. But if Naomi the hawk could destroy Gauguin's reputation a century after his death, what would she do to Witman if she found out about fourteen-year-old Violette? Maybe she could tell him now, just tell him, no one else. Maybe then she could persuade him to cancel her birthday party, which he was calling "A Roman Tribute to

Violette." Guy was sifting through Roman recipes, especially those of Apicius, the sad Roman, trying to find the perfect tribute for Violette's unwanted seventieth. No one was asking the birthday girl what kind of cake she wanted, just as no one was asking her how old she was.

4

The Transition

It is never a wise idea to keep a goat waiting.

Adara released the goat's still-bloated right udder, to be attended to later, and tilted the left one just so. As she squeezed, steamy, foaming milk squirted into her coffee mug with the bitter, sugar-sweetened, muddy Greek coffee at the bottom. The goat stammered a small protest as she worked. She sipped from the warm mug and, liking it, sipped again. She couldn't wait to tell Niki she had made a goat latte. No more visiting Little Italy for a demitasse or a cappuccino. Lattes had taken over the city. Though they wanted to keep up with the times, even Niki would not be able to talk the health inspector into it. But still, she thought, shouldn't they try it somehow? Wasn't that the kind of place they were creating? The goat started stamping her hind legs and Adara grabbed both udders,

one in each hand, and began pumping hot milk into the
bucket.

. . .

Violette was older than Art, but not by a lot. Just by enough
for her to seem what he called "womanly," an idea left over
from his adolescence that an older woman was more of a
woman. Of course, that had been when he was twelve and
the boys were talking about twenty-one-year-olds.

Still, older was more exciting to Art than taller (though
they both were intriguing, and he was drawn to women
who were taller than he even if it was just a trick of their
heels). After months of trying to casually stroll to Violette's
table and chat, at which he had none of Niki's skill, and
even after he'd introduced the root beer floats for her, Violette did not find him interesting. She could sense what he
wanted. You couldn't miss it in some men. He reminded
her of the ones she'd grown up with who tried to look
attractive in their volunteer fire department uniforms.
Once when Adara was in the restaurant she grabbed the
float, just out of curiosity, to take it to this woman who
always sat alone.

"This is something," thought Art. "A mano y mano
between the two most beautiful women in the world." He
liked the idea that one was dark-haired and the other light. It
could be like Ava Gardner and Grace Kelly fighting over
Clark Gable. Art wanted to be Gable. Adara was clearly sizing
up Violette, but Violette, ever since Sister Mary, did not feel
in competition with other women. She simply admired Adara,
whom she viewed as a truly beautiful woman.

Niki was only interested in his wife. Like most everyone else, he thought she was the world's most striking woman. Adara was not worried about Niki straying because, like him, she had the confidence of the beautiful. Adara, in the words of Tolstoy politely explaining the allure of Anna Karenina, was "full-bodied." Her black curved eyebrows and long curled lashes naturally endowed her with the look for which most women strive with makeup.

But she knew none of that was what held Niki. It was her goatish smell. This is not something that can be accomplished artificially. It wasn't that Adara smelled like a goat. But she had a natural perfume that resembled the one that gives goat milk its distinctive flavor, the reason it makes better cheese. On their island after rainfall, which was so rare that it was always greeted as a miracle, the whole island had that smell. A few people on the island always kept it. It may have had nothing to do with goats. Maybe it was just the earthen perfume of their home.

Back at the restaurant, Niki put his arms around Adara's "full body," brushed aside her thick dark hair, planted his nose on the whiskey-colored skin of her neck, and inhaled.

. . .

Ahh, the eighties! The rich who had retreated to the suburbs were coming back to town and were willing to pay for it. Now that Art had bought his first building, he saw opportunities everywhere. The mayor, the banks, they were all on Art's side. It had been a mistake that he was born on an island that had none. He belonged here, on this island, where the scent was one of money, not goats—at least to him.

Greek diners would not fit in here for much longer. They belonged to a different age. Art, at least in his mind, had already moved on from the Katz Brothers—even if it was still Niki and Adara's whole life. He was in the mood to buy. Acquisition. It was the American way. With the rents from his first building, he was soon able to open a small real estate office in midtown, which he kept furnished with a sumptuous leather coach and a blonde assistant—tall, of course.

Soon their Queens neighbor on the other side, Sam Golden, came to Art for advice. He was moving to Boca for the tax break and wanted to be out of his house well before April. Art was happy to buy it for less than a year's worth of his midtown office cost.

Now he was building his own little neighborhood in Queens and had an office in midtown with a blonde. Wasn't this perfect? Wasn't this the ideal portrait of a Manhattan landlord?

It was balding Art and not curly-topped Niki who was continually involved with different women—his "blondes," at least until their roots. What Art called blondes, though, Niki and Adara called Americans. All they meant was "not Greek." For a time Art was dating a Polish woman who was taller than he, even in bare feet. She too they called an American. Those were the two kinds of people. He did not bring his blondes to Queens so they would not have to face Adara's glare. Maybe someday if he dated a brunette he would bring her around. A brunette—why would he do such a thing?

Art would drive in every morning from Queens with his brother and sometimes his sister-in-law in his SUV. The smoked windows had been meant to give them the privacy of celebrities, and now Art felt like one. Everybody now knew who he was since no one else drove a car like this.

Parking was difficult but he did not want to "waste a fortune" on the Upper West Side parking garages. He was torn between disdaining them and entertaining the possibility of getting into that business, which was clearly going to grow with the transition. There was often an empty parking space across the street from the Katz Brothers. Horace, the doorman, occupied the spot next to it during his day shift. He held it until six P.M. when Felix, the night man, drove in from Astoria and took the spot. But the place in front of it, just across from the Katz Brothers, was empty. It was a moneymaker for the city: There was a No Parking sign, but it was hidden behind a leafy tree and so obscurely marked that no one saw it.

Rosita, who gave tickets, was always waiting. Everyone feared Rosita, though she was a pleasant-looking woman whose love of the mofongo served on Amsterdam was making her uniform so tight she no longer tried to fasten the upper two buttons (and even the third was a struggle). She said this gave men something to look at while she was ticketing their car. In some cases this was true.

Horace, a heavyset man with close-cropped hair that may have been gray, who filled out his doorman uniform with the look of a staff sergeant—a beefy look of authority beyond his position—would warn people that if they parked there, they would be towed. He warned Violette, who he had been told was a famous model. In fact, he found her parking spots. "See the blue one five cars down? She is leaving in twenty minutes." He had every space on the block monitored. Everyone wanted to park on West Eighty-Sixth Street so the doormen would look after their car. On the smaller streets they would be broken into.

Horace perfectly perceived the image Art was projecting and, unfortunately, he didn't like it. Anyway, the spaces weren't for landlords—they were for building staff and sometimes good tenants who remembered him at Christmas. When this new SUV parked in the trick spot, Horace said nothing. He even watched with some satisfaction as the car was towed away. The tow charge plus the ticket cost Art more than a burglary, and he was soon becoming a regular at the police garage on the pier off the West Side Highway.

. . .

With the rent from his new properties, and the banks eager to help, he was able to buy out Gonzalez's ever-scaffolded sixteen-story elevator building next to the Katz Brothers. Gonzalez still hadn't finished the renovations—he obviously hadn't had Art's vision—and he was anxious to sell at a low price because the building's apartments were mostly rent-stabilized and not profitable. Of course, what tenants called "affordable," landlords called "unprofitable." Often they really were profitable—they just made a small profit in a city where others were making large ones. In Manhattan it wasn't any fun to make a small profit. Art liked to say, "If the orchard is ripe, pick a lot of apples." West Eighty-Sixth Street was ripe.

Art could see that this new building was a waiting game. If a tenant's income rose above a certain level, the landlord could raise their rent. Art could raise it so high that the tenant would have to move and make room for someone who could afford it. This was how to arrive at "a fair market rate." Other tenants would probably just move away, and others would die. Dying was the more New York thing to do: No one willingly gave up a rent-stabilized apartment or a good parking spot. In fact, having them was a reason to stave off death.

Yes, by the late eighties the transition Art had envisioned was happening. To Art, the changes had begun when he started fixing up the old buildings. To Niki, it began when he saw that the raccoons were finally leaving. So both brothers were happy. But one night, sitting with Adara behind their house in Queens, Niki saw a raccoon and insisted that it had followed him from Manhattan.

Over the next few years, Art managed to strong-arm nearly all the old tenants out of the sixteen-story building. By 1990 his rents were so "fair" that he was making enough money to buy two more inexpensive buildings on the block. By then, everyone saw what was happening. West Eighty-Sixth Street was becoming one of the most expensive streets in Manhattan. To Art this was the fatalistic fulfillment of his destiny. He knew how much he was at cross-purposes: the people he was driving out of the Upper West Side were his regular customers. The diner was from the past and so were its patrons. The Katz Brothers, with its reddish fake-stone façade and cheap grilled cheeses, did not have a place in the neighborhood anymore.

. . .

Art could change tactics as easily as he could change nationalities. As gently as he could, he pointed out to Adara and Niki that if the restaurant was going to profit from the transition, they had to learn to "modernize." He declared that the diner was now to be called Mykonos. Their new restaurant was to offer what Art called a "modern international cuisine."

Art hired a new chef, Mario di Capri—no more from Capri than the Milanos were from Milan—who was said to be a three-star Italian chef, though they did not know who had given him those three stars. Adara would still supply the goat cheese. Niki would still be the greeter, only now he would be called the maître d'.

Before even opening, the label "modern international cuisine" had been scrapped. Art was now calling it "modern classical cuisine." To sell food, he reasoned, a new label had to be invented for it. A new century was coming, and a new Eighty-Sixth Street. Grossinger's landlord quadrupled their rent and the bakery was no more. Most everyone thought this was a sad moment, but Art thought the closing showed him that he had been right in not getting involved with the bakery. He was impressed with the landlord. If a man owned a property and rented it with short-term leases, he had the right to quadruple the rent. If the original tenants left, he could find someone else. If he could find someone to pay the higher rent, he had been right to raise it.

Art had to offer new food for the new century—not the old New York cheesecake or grilled cheese sandwiches. Special ingredients would be the key. Nothing would be ordinary. The scallops, dayboat scallops, would be sprinkled with saffron from Spain. The braised veal would be served with trompette de la mort—wild black mushrooms—and truffle oil. The lamb was to be grilled with wild garlic ramps. Grilled tuna was to be served with a pungent "Roman garum," a fermented fish sauce once popular in ancient Rome. The menu would explain the ancient history of garum. Art, expanding beyond rice pudding, delighted in making the garum from scratch, showing a flair for rotten fish.

Adara was enthusiastic about the change. Though it seemed a risk, running an evening restaurant would be much better than working the long hours of the diner. Art told Adara that in addition to cheesemaking, he had a special cooking task for her, one he said was for "the most important item on the menu." Her assignment was to make something called "Cato's cheesecake." The menu was to explain that this Roman recipe was the oldest known written recipe. Art knew cheesecake was popular but he didn't want a "loser cheesecake," the kind made by people who couldn't pay the rent. Adara resisted the idea of a Roman cheesecake. She argued that the first cheesecake had been Greek, but Art had done his homework. "Cato wrote his cheesecake recipe in 160 BCE," he argued, feeling that he sounded very professional as he said "BCE."

Adara was not to be intimidated. "Athenius wrote that there were cheesecakes a hundred years before that."

"But where are the recipes?"

"He said there were recipes, even books, on cheesecake."

"Where are they?"

"They're lost." She reflected for a furious moment and then announced, "My melopita is the recipe. It's older than Cato's."

"Cato's is the oldest cheesecake recipe. It is the oldest written recipe in existence. And for the first time since perhaps ancient Rome, we are going to make it—in our restaurant. Besides, who is Athenius?"

Adara snorted her disdain. "Ancient Rome. *Ancient Rome.* Ancient times begin with Greece!"

"And," Art said, pointing a finger in the air, "the cheesecake will be scented with truffle oil."

"Truffle oil?" said Niki and Adara.

"Yes, so it will have the scent of truffles."

"Who can smell truffles?" asked Niki.

"Very few people," conceded Art with great enthusiasm. "But the ones who can are the ones you want."

Niki and Adara, who knew little about truffles, looked at each other with uncertainty, but Art had tested his theory. He told them he had bought a black truffle, held it to his nose, and got a musty smell that resembled the shed on their island where old farm equipment was kept. Truffles were only embraced by people who have never had such a shed, he concluded.

"And I can assure you," Art boldly declared. "The people at the *New York Times* can smell truffles."

Art was excited about this idea. He would try it out on Violette.

"We are going to make an ancient Roman cheesecake," Art said to her one day as she sat at the counter alone. "What do you think of that?"

Sipping on her root beer, she said, "That sounds more like an idea for my husband."

Art, who had been looking for what he called a "wedge issue," said, "So you and your husband don't see these things the same?"

"We've never discussed cheesecake."

"Oh shit!" Art suddenly shouted, looking out the window, and he ran out of the restaurant, shouting, "Rosita! Wait. I'm moving it!"

5

The Big Event

It depends on who you're talking to, but for Masha Putz, this was the big event. For a long time her parents were afraid she would refuse to do it, but it turns out even rebels want to impress their peers. But she insisted on keeping things on her own terms.

To begin with, from an early age—as soon as she learned how to read the word "putz"—she refused to call herself "pootz." This was irritating to Saul, her father. Her mother, Sarah, was pigeon afficionado Ruth Arnstein's daughter, and she didn't care about such things. Arnsteins were tough in their own way. Sarah did not change her name when she married. Saul may have thought this was an insult, but he didn't want to sound sexist, so he never objected. But when Masha—Masha Arnstein Putz—would say, as she frequently did, "I'm just a Putz," Saul would get annoyed. Masha liked to watch Dad cringe.

This year, everyone in her class was having a bar or bat mitzvah. Bar mitzvahs were a competition. It was not so much the ceremonies, which were pretty much all the same, but the receptions. What kind of venue? What kind of food? Music? Any special guests? Jake Rubens claimed he was getting the pitcher Sandy Koufax, whom some of the kids had heard of, and even the ones who hadn't knew he was famous. He would be there signing autographs because Jake's father was "in base-ball." He'd never played baseball, but it was said that he was "in baseball." Not in baseball enough, apparently, because Koufax wouldn't do it, and they had to settle for Shawn Green, a big hitter, but an outfielder is a far cry from a starting pitcher. Besides, in this neighborhood, bar mitzvah kids want a Hall-of-Famer.

For Masha, her first big issue was the haftarah. She was to chant her selection in Hebrew. She wanted to pick her own. She wanted to read the part of Exodus when Moses comes back from receiving the law from God and finds the freed Hebrew slaves worshipping a calf. They must be punished. Masha was ready with her explanation: If the Hebrews are now free, they should be free to worship calves if they want. Moses tries to order them around because he claims he's talked to God, but we have seen people like that throughout history and must stand up to them.

Kids like Masha—there are not many of them, thank God—are a nightmare for rabbis, even progressive ones like Rabbi Noah Pinkerman. Saul's Modern Orthodox group would never work with Masha. Pinkerman supported women rabbis and performed gay marriages and was regularly invit-ing Palestinians to give talks in the synagogue, but this talk by Masha he would not know what to do with.

Fortunately the haftarah selection was supposed to correspond with the date of the event, and her choice was not the right one for her bat mitzvah. Masha protested but could not win. Even in a progressive synagogue there are some rules. And so Masha was stuck with this weird passage from Samuel in which Samuel, or Saul (her father's name, which Masha found an ironic coincidence), was instructed to slaughter people because they had been mean to the Hebrews as they were fleeing Egypt.

But Masha's main concern was that her reception had to be better than Rachel Rabbinowitz's. Rachel wouldn't have invited Masha to hers except to show off the wonder of her event. That was also why Masha invited Rachel. Besides, you could get in trouble with the school for excluding people. Masha's first boon was Diane Davis of the New York City Ballet. She was Masha's instructor at her ballet school and she'd agreed to attend and sign programs for anyone who was interested. She just wanted to celebrate Masha. Besides, Diane lived a lonely life apart from ballet and accepted most party invitations, even though she seldom ate at any of the events. Masha's class was not a ballet-loving bunch of kids, and Masha was not certain how many kids would care about a prima ballerina. But one would. It would kill Rachel Rabbinowitz. Rachel danced at the School of American Ballet, which Masha had failed to get into. Diane also taught there. So Rachel's teacher was coming to Masha's bat mitzvah.

After spending so much time at the Katz Brothers after school, Masha had imagined spectacular ice cream cakes for her own occasion. She never considered the fact that the diner was undergoing a transformation—nor that they had never done anything more elaborate than a scoop, anyway.

Well, two scoops. Grossinger's, which some say invented the modern ice cream cake, was gone. Luckily Masha's great advantage was that her father was a television producer. He immediately lined up Fabricio Bonatelli for a cooking demonstration. He would show the kids how to make gelati. Everyone could make their own gelato under the direction of the great Fabricio. Fabricio's television show, which Saul Putz happened to produce, was the most popular food show on television. He also owned restaurants in New York, Los Angeles, and Rome and was generally regarded as the nation's leading Italian chef. His trademark was shouting in a throaty voice, "Va bene! And here's your gelato. Va bene!"

This was better than the silly Katz Brothers ice cream. This was something. Rachel Rabbinowitz didn't have anything like it (although she'd had a famous French chef making crepes. Crepes. Who cares?). Saul also booked the WonTon Girls, who were not Chinese and had no connection to soup. They were teenagers, though considerably older than their fans. Masha's classmates loved the WonTon Girls and could tell apart the voices of the blonde, the redhead, and the girl with dyed purple hair. No one knew why they called themselves WonTon, and at every interview they gave a different explanation. They knew their business. Maybe their mystery was the reason they were so appealing to teenagers.

Saul Putz thought that they had a certain adult appeal as well, especially the one with purple hair, whose name was Becky—an unlikely name, he thought, for a sexy girl with purple hair. When she came to his office at the production company, which was more often than necessary, he would think about crossing boundaries. But Saul always stayed within them and wished Becky WonTon would stay out of his office.

This issue of boundaries was further inflamed by the sudden denunciation of Fabricio Bonatelli. Fabricio, who weighed nearly three hundred pounds, was an example of the lawlessness of mammals. Male birds and insects, even fish, know they have to be beautiful or females won't go near them. But male mammals feel entitled no matter what they look like. Fabricio, like an ugly billy goat, grabbed at whatever he liked. Saul knew he was infamous for harassing women in the kitchens of his restaurants. For a woman to get a good cooking position in a Bonatelli restaurant was an accomplishment that was rarely tossed away by complaining publicly. In the restaurants his employees knew why he hired attractive young cooks. But that was not what did him in. Donna Fontina, a production assistant at the studio, complained that he constantly squeezed her breasts. Saul admitted to himself that he frequently thought of squeezing Donna's ample and often well-displayed breasts and now, once again, saw the wisdom of restraint.

Masha's grandmother, Ruth Arnstein, called Fabricio a nogoodnik, which was a verdict from which there was no reprieve. She was the first of many to claim that Fabricio Bonatelli could not appear at Masha's reception. Masha was disappointed but her mother quickly agreed. Saul could not argue. His award-winning food show had been canceled. And so had the bat mitzvah appearance.

"Mario di Capri."

Masha glanced back at Saul with an empty stare as though he had just referenced something from a black-and-white movie.

"He is the chef at that new place on the corner."

"The Katz Brothers?" said Masha, desperately looking at her mother.

"It's not going to be a diner anymore. It's going to be really good when it reopens next month," Saul said to Masha.

But his wife said, "We should have dinner there before we book him. Or at least wait and see what the *Times* says. It's not like he's famous or anything."

"Yeah," said Masha. "Or infamous." But to herself she was pleased. For once she and Mom were thinking the same way. But before she could feel too good about it, Sarah added, "Let's see if they have a good ganache."

The whole family knew what that meant.

6

Greco-Roman New York Cheesecake

To Adara, Cato's cheesecake was still an absurdity. But Art would not accept her melopita. When she argued that it was better than Cato's recipe, Art said, "So make this one better. It takes a Greek to fix a Roman recipe."

This argument appealed to her.

She found a copy of Cato's book that had been translated into Modern Greek, or as she insisted, "the original Greek." But even in Greek the recipe was difficult to read. And how fortuitous that this edition skipped Cato's invectives against the Greeks and the Greek language.

"Metrokoites!" muttered Adara as she stared at the infuriating recipe. It was a word she did not use often, never publicly, because it was disrespectful to mothers. But after studying

Cato's recipe a little longer, she added a worse word that is disrespectful to goats.

Most New Yorkers might have thought the challenge was for her to make something as good as the traditional New York cheesecake. For Adara, the challenge was to be as good as her next-door neighbors' Sicilian cheesecake. But it quickly became clear that Cato wasn't competing.

He called it "placenta" and optimistically began, "Make placenta this way." Beyond this plain language almost nothing was clear. Emmer groats are soaked and mixed with "bread-wheat" flour to make a dough called "tracta." Then a cheese is made from curdling and draining sheep milk and mixing it with honey. So it was sweet? How much honey? Was this a dessert or a savory dish? Not a dessert, Adara decided. Not too much honey. Sicilians would have made it a dessert, but Romans? No. A savory side dish.

Time for the tracta—still not clear what it was. Cato said to roll it into sheets that were then dried in a basket. Metrokoites!

Oiled sheets of the tracta were to be layered with the sweet cheese over a base made of moistened flour set over oiled bay leaves. This was then covered with a heated crock, and cooked—over hot coals? "Be sure to cook it well and slowly." So is it grilled? Griddled? Broiled? Roasted? What would cooking it "well" be like? Isn't it all going to dry up? Still don't know what the tracta is.

She eventually realized that she could accomplish the whole process, soaking the emmer groats and all, by using a whole-wheat flour. After all, they were in America now. She mixed the flour with water and kneaded it with her bare hands until she had dough she could almost roll out. It was not very good dough, neither soft nor elastic. She kneaded it some more. Then, since she was in America, she tried again with an electric mixer for another hour. It was still not workable, so she added two eggs. This Roman had forgotten the eggs.

Then, as instructed, she rolled it out, dried it on racks, laid out the sheets of dough with a layer of cheese between them, and put it in the oven. She baked it at a low heat hoping it would be easier on the dough, but it came out tough—a brittle, unpleasant crust. This was not cooked well.

Then she realized the key that would unlock the recipe. Cato, like most men, needed a little help. This is why she, not Mario, had been given the cheesecake recipe. How many cheesecakes had Cato baked? Did he know how to bake at all? Probably not. A Roman man could only be rescued by a Greek woman. Since she was nowhere near Cato's grave, there was no way to know how disturbed his ghost might have been by this conclusion.

This time, after drying the tracta for a few hours, she submerged it in boiling water, but only for two minutes. This was still not right. She tried rolling the tracta much more thinly, and then only boiling for one and a half minutes. Of course she used goat milk, not sheep, which had been an obvious Roman mistake. Romans always overlooked their goats and fawned over sheep, a dumber, less gregarious companion, easy to rule. Romans sought conquest, not community. Adara curdled goat milk and drained it.

Cato called for bay leaf but, of course, bay leaf is inedible. Fennel. This recipe, whether it knew it or not, cried out for fennel. Wild fennel with yellow blossoms had grown uninhibited on her rocky native island. She grabbed a few bulbs from the walk-in refrigerator and finely minced them, then sautéed them, only for seconds, in hot olive oil. Then she poured anisette in the pan while it was hot and set it on fire. This mixture was blended into the cheese with a little freshly ground black pepper. She laid out a sheet of tracta and covered it with her cheese mixture, much lighter on honey than Cato's, then added two more layers. Cato said to place a final layer of tracta on top, which, of course, would dry out in baking. Instead, she grated on top a goat cheese that had been aged for six months.

Twenty minutes in a moderate oven was just enough to bake it together and melt the cheese. She carefully plucked oregano leaves from their stems and chopped the leaves from the ends of celery ribs. This mixture too was quickly tossed in hot oil and removed with a strainer in seconds, after the leaves had popped bright and crisp. She strained these bright emeralds and scattered them on the top of the cake. Cato said that the finished cake should be glazed in honey. Adara thought this was a terrible idea that would turn it into "a horrible sticky thing like some Turk might make." She looked at her confection like a painter deciding if a work is complete. It was. But Art, rather than admiring her work, wanted to add something. Adara feared it would be honey, but Art said, "What about the truffle oil?" It had to be a light touch, so Adara put the oil in an atomizer and misted the top for just the slightest scent.

Adara thought this cake was far too beautiful to be sliced. That night, she ordered twenty-four four-inch springform pans. She would make individual emerald-sparkling cakes— Cato's cheesecake, as their menu said, the oldest known recipe in the world. Art thought reviewers would like this deep sense of history. He also thought New Yorkers would like this deep sense of cheesecake. Niki and Adara thought the little cakes were beautiful. Art thought there was a scent of truffles.

One final touch before opening the new restaurant: That lady, Ruth Arnstein, had to stop feeding pigeons out front. Adara thought pigeons were harbingers of bad fortune; Niki thought they would attract raccoons. Art didn't mind the pigeons but he thought Ruth was a bad look—this heavyset woman with the bun of dyed auburn hair and the large Zabar's bag standing in front of their establishment. First they sent out Niki who, with his pleasant smile, told Ruth she had to stop because she was attracting raccoons. As he went back inside, Ruth stood where she was, contemplating this. She had never seen a raccoon and assumed this must be some kind of Greek myth.

Then out came Art, a man who always looked like he meant business because, in reality, he did. Ruth was not afraid of Art, even though he was now her landlord. He had bought her building, halfway down the other side of Eighty-Sixth, from an old-time retiring landlord who, according to Art, had no vision. Given her marginal income, Art could never raise Ruth's rent. Though she thought the neighborhood was losing its charm, "filling up with a bunch of pishers," she was never going to leave, even though she distrusted her new neighbors—people who were not New Yorkers, coming in from that vast wilderness known as "out of town." According to Ruth, they were Republicans, ate too much mayonnaise on everything, and were secretly anti-Semites.

She had only left New York City once and never would again. She had visited a friend's summer home upstate as a teenager. While there, a twelve-year-old boy had been struck by lightning and killed. It was said that he was struck because he was in an open field with no tall trees or buildings to draw the electricity away. That was when Ruth realized that Manhattan was the only safe place to be. She would just avoid neighborhood rooftop parties. She gained further evidence that "out-of-town" was unsafe when Leonard, her husband, was killed by a truck in a rental car on the Long Island Expressway. Leonard had been a wholesaler of asparagus and artichokes. Ruth never understood why anyone would wholesale only these two vegetables, but he had earned a satisfactory living for her and their daughter, Sarah. It did not take a huge income in the neighborhood to get by in those days and there was a whole community, a landsleit, Ruth used to call it, of middle-income people supporting each other there. After Leonard died, Ruth was safe because he had left enough money for her to live simply in a rent-stabilized apartment. Sarah had married a television producer and was well taken care of, so Ruth had nothing to fear from this Greek.

Art told Ruth that he did not want her feeding the birds in front of his restaurant. Before walking away she said, "I know you are all excited about this new thing you're doing, but you are going to find that some birds are just here to stay."

7

Mimi's Home

To Mimi Landau, the name Cato did not evoke cheese-cake. Mimi knew everyone else in the neighborhood, or at least everyone on the block. She met many of them walking Cato. Cato was her black standard poodle who wanted to hug everyone, so everyone loved him in return. Dogs understand that this is how it works. It works this way for people too, but they often don't understand. There were a few who didn't want Cato's hugs, but it was Mimi's conviction that one should avoid anyone who didn't want to be hugged by a poodle. If you brushed the thick black curls out of his face, you could see the penetrating olive brown eyes of a philosopher—the kind of eyes that could see through anyone. That is why Mimi named him Cato, although the Roman Cato had not really been a philosopher. She just hadn't liked the name Plato because it sounded too much like Pluto.

Cato was a perfect match for Mimi's black outfits. Now they had a collective identity. She and Cato knew everyone and they knew everyone's dogs. Even when Mimi didn't remember the name of the person, she always knew the name of the dog. Then, at age fourteen, Cato died for no particular reason. Mimi was left bereft and without any purpose for her walks. Some blows in life are just a bad turn. Others are the beginning of everything going wrong. Sometimes the world gangs up on you—there is no mistaking it.

· · ·

For the lucky people who got invited to one of Mimi's parties, it was like being invited to a private museum. Mimi loved throwing these events, but now, as she set out dishes and tidied up for guests, she knew this was to be her last one. Her apartment had always been an expression of her life. This is true of many people's homes, but Mimi had an unusual life and, for now, an apartment to show it.

She was supposed to have been a biologist. She always said that. After earning a biology degree from Columbia University, she had worked in a laboratory that studied viruses. There she met Arnold Litvak, a brilliant biologist. His work on flu strains had saved lives and it was often rumored that he was to receive a Nobel Prize, but Sweden had remained silent. Arnold had shoulder-length hair and wore flowered shirts. Mimi also had shoulder-length black hair but with a thick flow to it, whereas Arnold's was scraggly. Mimi was always lean and fit, a gift she had not entirely earned with her half-hour of home exercises every morning. Her fitness seemed emphasized by her habit of always wearing nothing but black. They had suited each other, looked right together, looked like a couple.

They married and their lives were filled with discoveries. They rented a large apartment on the top of a building on West Eighty-Sixth Street, not far from their work at Columbia. A biologist could afford such things then. She became fascinated by the alchemy of baking, the impact of salt and eggs and butter and, most especially, yeast. She had built her dream kitchen, the kitchen she imagined, with large industrial stoves, baking racks, and a large oak-and-marble island (brushed stainless steel had not yet come into fashion), and a chubby wooden chopping block, which every kitchen in New York was getting from antique shops at the time. The rack of knives and cleavers was as well-laid as a surgeon's tools.

Then a project connecting DNA, the new cutting edge of biology, to susceptibility to certain viruses went wrong and was dismissed as a failure when Arnold accidentally infected himself and died. For the rest of her life, no matter what she worked on, in his honor she always referred to herself as a biologist. She left the laboratory and began selling pastries to restaurants. Her business was called Biology Pastry, which was perhaps not the best marketing image, but customers liked what she sold. She would go to the Hungarian bakeries on Seventy-Second Street to get ideas, sitting with her friend Ruth in the old Éclair, listening to the singsong Yiddish arguments of older men. Mimi ordered the poppyseed strudel but, really, her favorite was the cheesecake. After her husband died Ruth never ordered cheesecake again because it had been his favorite. It was a matter of respect.

Gradually, Mimi's business became a full-range catering service, and by chance she became a popular caterer for art programs, through which she came to know many gallery owners and artists. Though she had no background in art (nor in baking), she thought she could use her contacts with galleries to promote the art she liked. She had strong opinions on art, and by now she looked more like an artist than a biologist. Her black clothing contrasted with her hair, which had become silver. Her only jewelry was a deeply lustrous white pearl, the only piece of jewelry Arnold ever gave her. Working in a laboratory, they had not believed in rings. Later Mimi concluded that pastry makers, artists, and musicians should not wear rings either. He had given her the pearl with great excitement, explaining that it was artificial and a work of brilliant engineering. That was Arnold, always preferring the interesting to the valuable. It was one of the few things that she had from him. Her habit of acquisition came after he was gone, when life had a different kind of energy and she had a lot of space to fill.

During her catering days, Mimi met a young artist from the Caribbean island of Trinidad, Lewiston St. Jean, whose strong brushstrokes in wild colors looked abstract but, in his mind anyway, were figurative, with titles such as *The Vegetable Vender*, *Dogfight*, and *Chickens Home to Roost*. Mimi started inviting gallery owners and critics to six-course dinners at which she introduced them to the artist and his work. She also hosted music nights in which eight musicians were brought in to perform Bach cantatas. She had a Steinway grand piano that was said to have once belonged to Arthur Rubenstein.

Her evenings became famous. Musicians wanted to play chamber music for her. Artists wanted to show paintings. Everyone wanted to eat her food. Lewiston St. Jean's paintings were starting to sell. And then, just as she was feeling ready to take her relationship with this young and brilliant man to what she called "the next tier," he disappeared. It seemed to Mimi that there was some kind of lesson in this, though she was not sure exactly what it was. He really vanished without any note or explanation. He shared no more paintings and no one ever heard from him again, including the gallery that had launched him. They sold everything. There was no more. He never collected the money.

In the hallway leading to the kitchen she had an original set of pieces of his: five four-color woodcuts depicting various cakes and pastries she had made. St. Jean called them *Just Desserts*. She had been offered substantial sums of money for them, but though the offers kept increasing, she thought she would never sell. Of course, now, maybe she would.

She collected both art and artists. No Witmans, of course, even if he was in the neighborhood. Too expensive. Maybe she resented his prices, but she and Ruth went to the show at the Whitney years ago and they were not impressed. They thought there was something vaguely sexist about the work. "Girly pictures," Ruth had sneered.

But Mimi said, "Girly but painterly."

Her brief affair with a Catalan abstractionist who only worked in black, gray, and brown left her with three large works on her wall after he departed. *Why should I be surprised*, Mimi thought to herself. *The man had no color.* She collected other Spanish abstracts with bigger names—Chillida, Tàpies,

Guerrero, and Saura. She had a large glass piece by the West Coast artist Chihuly that hung from her high ceiling and tinkled as the kitchen door opened to announce the coming of food. She also had a nearly life-size bronze calf encrusted with blue sapphires (or so she was told) that she had bought on a trip to India. The bronze had tarnished to become dark, but the nose was a bright gold because she rubbed it for luck every time she left the apartment.

A trapeze hung in her spacious living room. Mimi claimed that she had been a trapeze artist as an adolescent and said that she could still swing hanging from her ankles, but she never demonstrated. No one believed she had ever really been a trapeze artist. A few guests dared her to perform a trick or two. She wouldn't, but she did have a pinball machine on which she had maintained some astounding skills of her youth.

Then Art Katsikas bought out Mimi's building and her neighbors started to leave. The pleasant-looking Greeks reminded Mimi of that famous line from Baudelaire, "Where evil comes up softly like a flower." She'd always liked Baudelaire. In a formerly middle-class building, none of the old-time tenants could pay the new rents. There were always richer people available in Manhattan, many from out of town, since people from all over the world come to New York to be rich. The old New Yorkers who had characterized the neighborhood—social workers, teachers, magazine writers—were being driven out. An actress who had the misfortune of five successful commercials taking her income over the limit for rent stabilization had to move, though she might never work again. They all left for parts unknown, fearing there would be no affordable apartments left in Manhattan. Art had no sentimentality about old tenants the way a longstanding business might for its longtime customers.

These New Yorkers were replaced by fair-haired out-of-towners (it was not true, as Mimi always insisted, that all of them were blond—New Yorkers always imagine out-of-towners as blond) who worked for banks, investment houses, stock brokerages, insurance companies, and prestigious law firms. Many had become rich doing things that were incomprehensible. Who really knows what a hedge fund is? Mimi always confused it with hedge*hog*, though she didn't know what a hedgehog was either except in Isaiah Berlin's philosophical essay. These new out-of-towners—pishers, according to Ruth—were armed with the new Walkman cassette players that the new tenants held with increasing fascination. One of them would step into a full elevator with his headphones on and say nothing. Then he would step out on the ground floor (no women or elderly first to think about) and walk through the lobby with his Walkman (the yellow "sports" model if he was going running) stuck out in front of him, without a word to the doorman holding the door. This one actually had a leather holster at his hip for the Walkman and he sauntered off with his piece drawn like Jesse James silently heading for the bank job. They were all young and in many cases had several babies. They were only staying in the building until they found their perfect, very large co-op, so their apartments changed tenants every six months and, though the landlords had to refurbish, each change allowed Art another hike in the rent. The building, instead of being a community of landsleit, became a stopover for transients.

Some of the true old-timers had to be clever to avoid wealth. Ti Auguste had lived in the building for more than forty years, from back when living was cheap and you could buy a Creole newspaper on the corner. He dared not sell his paintings at a gallery for the prices they could command. Instead he sold them for modest prices out of his home.

It was through Ti Auguste that Mimi had become interested in Haitian art. She had two small bronzes by Georges Liautaud and a large piece by Serge Jolimeau, who was from the same town. She had decided to write a book on the subject. There were not many books on it, but she reasoned that perhaps not that many people were interested. Besides, art books never make much money. There had been no way to predict that the book would earn her $250,000 in one year. But there was no reason to panic. Sales had dropped by the end of the year and the book appeared to have run its course. No. The second year, the book, which had become required reading in art schools and universities, earned even more, pushing her just over the threshold for a rent increase.

Mimi, who was forced to submit her income each year to the landlord, was finished. And the IRS said they wanted to audit her taxes, probably because they couldn't believe the sudden rise and fall of her income. Then her dentist said she needed an implant that cost thousands but that insurance would not cover. Without it, she would have the gap-toothed look of a homeless person, which she might soon be. The way things were going, it came as no surprise when she was contacted by the Greeks, as she called her landlords, who informed her that she was officially losing her rent stabilization. Her rent was going to be raised dramatically to "fair market price." She would never have another year in which she could pay this new "fair" price. That markets would be fair is the foundational lie of capitalism.

She ran her fingers through her hair, a dramatic white against her black clothing, and looked around. She'd have a last party, one last lustrous evening in her palace. But then what was she going to do with all this *stuff*?

8

Cato's Launch

They each had their own concerns. Niki, whose world was ordered by scents like a well-bred hound, understood that for a restaurant to succeed, it had to have the right smell. Why? The customer, he explained, sits down and he feels content and he is ready to eat. It is not the tablecloth or the soft lighting or artwork on the walls. It is the scent.

Niki toured restaurants all over Manhattan, sniffing. They did not smell alike, but all the best ones were pleasing. What would the smell of Mykonos be? Onions, even though they were common. Niki insisted that one burner of their stoves always had to be reserved for a skillet of caramelizing onions. At home he had noticed that if he was sautéing onions when dinner guests arrived, they would invariably say, "Something smells good." But that was not enough. Bunches of fresh rosemary were hung from the ceiling as had been done in their parents' kitchens. Bowls made from knotty olive wood were rubbed with olive oil. But something was still missing. What? Despite Art's advice, he had to admit that he could not smell truffles and so suspected that no one else could either. "The *New York Times* can smell it," Art countered.

No, thought Niki. It would not be truffles, because that would make the restaurant smell like an old shed. The restaurant needed the scent of goatishness. Niki brought in Adara's fresh goat cheeses and put them out in bowls of green olive oil—a peppery nectar from the southern Peloponnese where the olives were cold pressed in baskets so that the oil was like green liquid fruit. Any knowledgeable food writer will explain that color does not determine the taste and fragrance of olive oil, but anyone who knows olive oil knows that green is the best. The cheese in green olive oil was there for the ambiance, not to be eaten, and it occurred to Niki that this might have been what Cato had in mind with his odd cheesecake. But now that Adara had worked out a dish that Art was excited to sell, Niki didn't share this subversive thought.

Now they were ready.

The day of the opening, Adara peeled a white onion and the three passed it, each taking a large bite, like ancient Olympians building strength for an upcoming contest. Opening night went well, and so did the next one. Customers seemed to enjoy Mario's food—and Niki was irresistible. They were filling the small restaurant, which did not take a great many people. They took in three times as much money per day as the diner had when it was full. The important point, for Art, was that it was hard to land a table and reservations had to be made days in advance.

The customer they wanted, the one they needed, Amy Artina, had not appeared. Amy Artina was the *New York Times* restaurant critic. No one knew what she looked like. She always used a false name and, it was said, many disguises. Sometimes she was an exotically overdressed Latina, or an Italian in fur who seemed to be an opera star, or a provincial Midwestern tourist. She never came as a regular New Yorker because that was what she was. So when New Yorkers turned up, which was most of the time, the Katsikases did not need to fuss. Besides, Niki lit up for everyone.

That night, two weeks after opening, Mykonos had a reservation under the name Putz. When the guests arrived to claim the reservation, he in an Armani suit and she in a stylish dress of unknown origin, Art recognized Mr. Putz. Saul didn't mind the way Art said "putz" and didn't correct his pronunciation because he was pretty sure Art didn't know what a putz was.

To Art, Saul was a man of disguises, but he certainly wasn't Amy the critic, and the woman with him, with a big diamond ring, looked so much like what Art imagined Saul's wife would be that she could not possibly be a food critic in disguise. Art had seen Saul on the street with other men, wearing black hats or sometimes skull caps. He never dressed that way in their restaurant. The Orthodox thing was a hobby for Saul, but this year he was much more interested in the other synagogue and Masha's bat mitzvah. The Orthodox men didn't even think girls should have bat mitzvahs so Masha didn't like them. Saul and his wife were here to check out the new chef, Mario di Capri, before hiring him to cook at Masha's big event.

"Please, this way, Mr. Putz," said Niki.

"Pootz," Saul couldn't help saying, though he did not think this one knew what a putz was either.

"Saul Pootz," and he handed him a business card that said he was the producer of the Fabricio show, the hottest food show on television. This card was generally his ticket to a good table and top treatment at any restaurant. But everyone already knew the show had been canceled. Besides, he was a customer from the diner, which gave him low standing. Mr. Putz would not get the best table. The Greeks could see that these were not food critics. Food critics don't flash cards and try to get good tables. He was all polished and decorated and didn't fool anyone.

Just then, A. G. Hoffman and his wife arrived. Hoffman always made reservations with the A. G. because that had been his byline and he thought it would get him a better table. But, in truth, since no one remembered A. G. Hoffman anymore the initials got him nothing. Besides, Art recognized him from his tuna sandwiches and was not happy. Too many from the old diner were showing up. These were not the *Times* critics. Art also thought he might have seen this man leave the diner with Serafina one night. He could be wrong. Regardless, these weren't the people the Greeks were looking for. Niki ushered the couple to their seats.

"Tell me," Hoffman said to Niki. "What rhymes with cheesecake?"

"What rhymes with . . . I'll have to think about it." And he quickly moved on.

Adara said that Artina was a Greek name and that all they had to do was look for a Greek in disguise, an old Trojan warning. Niki pointed out that the Greek name was Artino, not Artina. But Adara was certain. Art thought Amy Artina sounded Jewish. But Niki said it didn't matter because Jews look Greek anyway. He cited the example of the movie star Omar Sharif.

"But he's Egyptian," Art protested. Niki brushed away his hand and said, "Same thing."

. . .

That night, the best table was probably going to go to the couple reserved under the name Balaska. They had known Belaskos in Athens. In any event, the name had gotten their attention when the reservation was made days earlier. "Who are the Balaskas?"

When the guests arrived for their two-top, Niki led them with a smile to the best table. There was not a great difference in the tables—nearer the counter, nearer the window (though Eighty-Sixth and Columbus was not a scenic view). But it was important to have a table designated in their own minds as "the best."

The Balaskas were large women, not fat but sizable. They looked well fed the way Americans often do. They spoke with the twang of an untuned banjo, their voices suggesting large fields and blue skies, something more expansive than New Jersey. Niki was suspicious because he did not think anyone really spoke this way. They were much more talkative than New Yorkers should be, and by the time they were seated he already knew that they were tourists, had gone to the Guggenheim Museum, and had seen two musicals on Broadway. New York is an immigrant city. You just don't give out information like this. This kind of openness to strangers is not the New York way. They said they came from Indiana, from a town called French Lick. They giggled about the name and waited for Niki to do the same.

He giggled. Niki knew how to giggle when he had to.

They explained that the town was named after a salt lick. They also said that wine was made there and that Larry Bird, the basketball star, had been born there. But since he played for Boston this was not something that earned points in New York. Niki, still smiling anyway, laughed to himself. He was sure there was no basketball player named Bird. These *New York Times* people with their fake accents and disguises are having fun.

The evening skated on—graceful turns and spins, no jumps or flips. The Putzes were arguing over whether garum was kosher. Not that it mattered since they never tried to eat kosher. They were just interested in the question. Saul loved the rabbinical pose. Using both the voice tones and hand gestures that he had seen on rabbis, Saul explained that the central question was how the fermentation is started. They wanted to call Niki over to question him on it, but Niki focused on the "women from Indiana."

The women seemed increasingly taken with Niki's charm. The one that he thought was Amy seemed as though she was ready to abandon the *Times* and run off with him. It must be lonely, being a restaurant critic. They ordered the tuna and the lamb, which Adara thought were good choices. Niki recommended they pair it with Mavrotragano, a deep red wine from the volcanic slopes of Santorini. Niki understood that there was nothing sexier than a man who knew dark, velvety reds.

Then Niki brought them two Cato's cheesecakes. Adara had prepared them carefully, arranging the bright fried leaves in perfect casual display and spraying the truffle oil generously in case Art was right. Niki did the whole presentation: how the recipe comes from the oldest book of Latin prose, how it is the first written recipe. How it is a very difficult recipe that his wife, a classics scholar, spent months deciphering. The trick of lying well is to mix it in with truth. No one will be able to sort it out.

Art listened closely because he wanted to give the same learned presentation to Violette and her husband, who were seated at the next table. So *that* was her husband. He looked much older. But he had great hair. She probably liked a man with good hair, Art thought. The husband, whose insipid name turned out to be Guy—*Guy?*—leaned over his dish and flipped his long hair behind him, a no-hands trick he obviously took pride in. As Violette predicted, he took great interest in the cheesecake and started grilling Art about its authenticity. "Well, all recipes are a matter of interpretation," said Art with a broad smile and soft eyes. It amused Violette to realize that Art was trying to imitate his brother.

Guy prattled on about Cato's Rome and even quoted Cato in Latin.

This guy is a putz, thought Art. *She is probably tired of him and looking for something different, someone younger and more exciting.* Art tried to convince himself that he was exciting. He owned a lot of real estate now.

Guy asked him for the recipe but Art would not give it out. "We are having a big party and we would like to serve this," Guy said, as though bestowing an award.

"We can cater your party," Art offered.

"We like to do things for ourselves," said Guy, flipping back his mane.

Yes, he is a putz, Art thought.

Niki remained focused on the *New York Times* Hoosier ladies.

One of them had eaten the entire cake and one left half. He supposed Amy was the one who left half. If you eat for a living you can't eat everything. He offered them dessert. Mario had prepared a list, several including figs. One was simply goat cheese and figs. Niki, following instructions, pointed out that figs were a favorite of Cato's, which was sort of true. Adara wondered why he hadn't put figs in his cheesecake. That might have been a good idea. Cato couldn't cook.

Art noticed Violette and Guy arguing about something. He thought it might be their party. Maybe the cheesecake. They didn't get along.

Everyone ate well and Niki led them each to the door, sated ruminators coming from the pasture in burpy contentment. Saul Putz, impressed with the new restaurant, was thinking of a Cato cheesecake for the bat mitzvah, but his wife wisely suggested, "Let's see what the *Times* says. I think it needs ganache."

The two women "from Indiana," content with their cheesecake, passed on the desserts. As Niki walked them to the door, one of the women looked like she was about to pounce on him, tear at his clothing and beg him to run away with her to French Lick where they could be winemakers together. But Niki knew how to get away with just a warm goodbye. This was partly because he understood that there was no such place as French Lick and that he simply had to wait for tomorrow's review.

. . .

When the *Times* review by Amy Artina came out, the Katsi-kases sat around the newspaper in Adara's kitchen in Queens. Niki felt confident. Immediately Art grinned when she praised "the newest thing: modern classical cuisine."

"At first I was skeptical," wrote Amy. "But dishes like tuna in a sharp and briny fermented fish sauce . . ." Art was triumphant again ". . . and Cato's cheesecake made me believe." She devoted two paragraphs to the cheesecake—to the idea and to the cake.

"Chef Mario di Capri's artful resurrection of the world's oldest written recipe, a bejeweled savory masterpiece . . ." Adara's dark eyes for a moment turned even darker. But then she smiled. They all smiled. They had made the transition.

There was only one criticism. There is always one. Critics think they need to have one—always irritating, like a splinter too small to locate. Amy wrote, "The service was inattentive and indifferent. It's a new restaurant and perhaps this will improve in a few weeks."

"What more could I have done?" Niki pleaded, palms up toward the gods.

"I don't know," said Art with a mischievous grin. "Did you have to keep your clothes on?"

. . .

A letter came from French Lick, Indiana. Yes, it turned out that there really is a French Lick, Indiana. It also seemed likely that the *New York Times* restaurant critic didn't live there. But now it seemed that somebody else really did. She wrote on the kind of engraved stationery used by a woman who was in the habit of sending letters by mail. And, of course, whoever it was remembered his name.

Dear Nicky,

We wanted to thank you for being so kind and attentive . . .

(*So SHE thought I was attentive*, thought Niki.)

. . . when we ate at your wonderful restaurant. It really was the high point of our trip to New York.

One small criticism . . .

(*Here it is*, thought Niki. *Everyone is a critic.*)

. . . when an Indiana girl goes to New York, she looks forward to the cheesecake. Yours was not what we were expecting. Would you consider some fruit on top—maybe cherries or strawberries?

With fond regards from your Hoosier friends,

Alice and Patty

9

Cheesecake Outbreak

Within months, cheesecake was sprouting in shaded corners of West Eighty-Sixth Street like mushrooms in a humid forest—and, like mushrooms, it was important to know which ones to pick. Once Amy Artina of the *New York Times* gave her blessing, everyone wanted to offer Cato's Eighty-Sixth Street cheesecake. The donut shop featured a cheesecake donut. It had a honey glaze so it could be argued that it was more authentic than Adara's. But this was a coincidence. The donut makers never read Cato's recipe, which would only have seeded confusion. A new little macaron shop selling delicately colored filled meringues offered a sleeve with all the flavors: brown for chocolate, tan for espresso, yellow for lemon, orange for mandarin, green for green tea, pink for raspberry, or purple for cheesecake.

The shop had recently been opened by Janet Margolis, a long-faced, serious Culinary Institute of America graduate commonly known as Jay Mac, after she had opened five macaron shops elsewhere in the city. This was the first to offer the cheesecake flavor. Jay Mac knew how to work her way into a neighborhood, and this was now Cato's neighborhood. The cheesecake macaron was purple because she vaguely recalled, from that misty education before cooking school, that purple was the color of Roman aristocrats (although she was not certain that Cato was an aristocrat). She regularly took cheesecake macarons to Horace, the doorman. Horace always had a parking spot for her.

The purple ones were the most popular, just as the cheesecake filling was the most popular in the donut shop. Violette had heard that Jay Mac was selling violet-colored cheesecake meringues and wanted to know why. It was bad enough that Guy was now telling everyone that he was making an "authentic" Cato's cheesecake for her unwanted birthday party.

"Why is the cheesecake violet-colored?" Violette asked.

Jay Mac politely explained, "Because cheesecake is Roman and purple is a Roman color."

Violette, feeling herself slip into another conversation about Roman history and culture—there had been quite a few of them lately—wanted to step off. "Do you have any cold drinks?"

"No. There are no cold drinks," said Jay Mac in a tone that seemed a reprimand.

Violette, unimpressed, pushed on. "What you really need here is to offer root beer floats. You see, if you had a root beer float, I would come in, get the drink, and buy a few sleeves of macarons."

Jay Mac had no answer. Violette walked out and continued her morning.

Mimi Landau and Ruth Arnstein were slowly making their way to the macaron shop. A shop like this opening on their block was a bad omen. Was this becoming the sort of neighborhood that had macaron shops? The women's progress was slow for a number of reasons. Mimi was in no hurry to get there. But walking with Ruth was always slow because she chatted and distributed dollar bills to the homeless and Milk-Bones to the dogs, who pulled on their owners' leashes to greet her.

Now the women were particularly slow because, since her hip operation, Ruth had been using a walker. The problem had been caused by Bailey (people who aren't Jewish name their dogs Bailey), a powerful lab who had jumped on her and knocked her over a pile of bags gathered by a homeless man whose name even Ruth didn't know. It seemed an accident specially designed for her. Wasn't that just like Ruth?

Except that it wasn't true. Fiction is often more credible than the unlikely facts. Ruth didn't hurt her hip by being knocked over by an overly loving or anti-Semitic Labrador retriever (depending on who was telling the story). Actually, the accident had happened in Mimi's apartment. Ruth had been teasing her about the trapeze. "You weren't ever a trapeze artist, were you?"

"No, I really was."

"Do something."

"Oh, no. I don't do it anymore."

"Right, I bet you never did. Here, I'll do something." She shoved over a stepladder and climbed into a sitting position on the bar, pulling with her arms and kicking with her legs, the way she had on the swings in Central Park when she was a little girl. It made her happy as she swung ever higher—and then just slid off the bar like a Flying Wallenda, sailing across the room and into the Chillida lithograph, the thick black circles and bars being the last thing she saw as she passed out from the pain of a broken hip. Even now she feels the pain. When she does, the image of that Chillida fills her vision.

It irritated her that her building was one of the few on the block where there were steps by the doorway—just two marble steps into the lobby that were difficult to negotiate with a walker. The doorman had to help her into the marble mausoleum of an entryway. The walls were flesh-colored marble and the floors were large flesh-and-black colored tiles in geometric patterns with ochre-and-black tile borders suggesting rugs. It was reminiscent of the floors of a Renaissance palazzo—but really more suggestive of an Upper West Side apartment building since so many of them had this kind of flooring. The building staff would keep it polished and complain that Ruth was scuffing the floor with the walker and needed to get better rubber tips for it.

She hated the walker because she could see people looking at her slyly and thinking *That's it for Ruth Arnstein*. She did not feel that her days were numbered, though it could be argued that everyone's days are numbered. It's just that no one knows the number. The macaron shop was on the side of the street with the lumpy sidewalk, making the walk to the shop even slower.

Ruth thought it would be a fine thing if they could get homemade macaroons from the neighborhood, rather than the boxed industrial ones, for her granddaughter Masha's bat mitzvah. Ruth thought half should be chocolate-dipped and the others plain coconut. She was speaking loudly as she often did outside because she was usually accompanied by the flutter of bird wings. When they walked into the macaron shop, Ruth wasted no more time. "Where's the coconut?"

Jay Mac was perplexed. She explained her repertoire of flavors while Ruth shook her head *no* to each one. "You don't understand," said Ruth, trying to be patient, something that she never quite achieved. "It's my granddaughter's bat mitzvah and I wanted to bring macaroons."

"Why don't you bring cheesecake macarons? They are very popular."

"No," said Ruth in a disheartened tone. "Someone else is doing the cheesecake. I don't eat cheesecake."

Mimi ushered her out the door before she could explain why she didn't eat cheesecake anymore. They continued on their slow journey. In days gone by they had gone over to Columbus for marbled cheesecake or, in Ruth's case, because she didn't eat cheesecake anymore, Hungarian rigó jancsi—or in the fall when plums were ripe, German pflaumenkuchen. But the Hungarians were all gone from Columbus. There was only a Gap, a chain store where on principle Mimi and Ruth refused to buy clothes. The last Hungarians on Amsterdam had been driven out of business too.

At least they could always rely on breakfast at Barney Greengrass around the corner. Barney Greengrass had cheese-cake for Mimi and lox and bagels for Ruth. Yet Ruth's ability to eat lox, too, was in jeopardy after her lox-loving brother was killed, hit by a bus at Eighty-Sixth and Columbus. The death of Benny Arnstein had raised considerable consterna-tion in the neighborhood because, while most people who'd been killed in that crosswalk had been hit by taxis cutting the corner from Columbus, this was a bus coming straight on. Ruth and Benny had not been close but one thing she did know about him was his favorite food, effectively eliminating lox and bagels from Ruth's diet once he had died. But Mimi argued to Ruth with the finesse of a big law firm partner that her brother had specifically loved nova, the lightly cured favorite of 90 percent of the customers at Barney's. Ruth could just eat the salty belly lox instead. Just as long as it was not on his preferred onion bagel.

As time went on, as Ruth would lose more and more people, she feared her diet would become increasingly limited. No cheesecake was already bad enough. Mimi ordered a slice.

10

Roman Reality

Sabino Begotxu, the celebrated metal sculptor, was excited about working in cheesecake. Guy had come to him with the idea of sculpting one for Violette's birthday party. He was to use a recipe from ancient Rome. Sabino, who famously opposed the commercialization of art, could envision it. He would build a postmodern classical building in cake—cubes and angular blocks adorned by Doric columns. The party would be full of curators and critics who would declare the cake "Sabino's greatest masterpiece." Then they would all eat it.

Sabino, like his sculptures, was cubic. He had a thick muscular square body and a cube-like head with a square jaw. Even his dark, deep-set eyes looked like black dice. He looked as though he had sculpted himself. Whenever he saw Violette he would tell her how much he wanted to sculpt her, too. Guy thought it would be interesting to see the cubic metal version of his wife. But Sabino never did sculpt Violette and probably never would. He had one large public piece in Buenos Aires that had won a major international award, and his reputation rested almost entirely on that. He did gift a piece to Violette and Guy that was in their garden: two bronze cubes with slightly slanted surfaces so that the two related to each other differently from every possible angle. Sabino said it was his comment on relationships. He was not married.

Guy had once visited Sabino's studio in San Sebastián and the floor had been so littered with dusty metal pieces that it was difficult to walk. His work had not been for sale. Now he could present the art world with the new work they had all been asking for. And it would be edible. He laughed to himself.

A few weeks before the party, Sabino came by the penthouse to plan the cake. Guy, in his favorite white apron, was bent over a marble pastry board next to Violette.

"Guy," said Sabino. "I need to talk to you about something."

Guy looked up with clear gray eyes that seemed to see through everything.

"I don't get it," Sabino said. "Do not get it. Is it the emmer? Tracta, he calls it. What is tracta? I husk the emmer to make groats. I mix them with water, get it nice and soft like he says. I knead it. I mix it with flour. Roll it into sheets. Dry them out. Press them with cloth and maybe soak in oil. But it is still going to be as hard as Sheetrock."

Guy said, "I think the historians are right. The ones that say you aren't supposed to eat it. Although sheep cheese is really good. We don't need to eat it—let's just burn it as an offering. Just at the moment that we all wish Violette a happy birthday, I'll set it on fire. Roman cheese fireworks. The oil in the dough will help."

Sabino liked this idea. He would sculpt something that would look dramatic in flames. If this worked well he might do others. Flaming Begotxus.

Of course, this was not what anyone else had in mind (except possibly Cato). Still, there was considerable excitement about Sabino sculpting Cato's cheesecake, and the guests were sure to arrive with their appetites whetted by the promise of a cheesecake like no other. They had read the *Times*.

.   .   .

The building's two elevators only held eight people at a time, so a crowd was forming in the lobby. It was dark like an ancient castle, with thick wooden beams across the ceiling and lit by inefficient chandeliers with many small bulbs. The furniture was ornate, Louis-the-something, and looked as though you were not supposed to sit on it. In any case no one did. There was a dark, tall block-like stand, oversize, that looked like something from Kafka's *Trial*, and behind it stood a uniformed doorman who was clearly in charge.

Hoffman was glad to have been invited. In the old days he was invited to everything, but he didn't get invited much anymore. Amy, who knew him from the *Times*, occasionally invited him to restaurants she was reviewing, but he knew that was because no one remembered or even noticed him. He had seen Violette and Guy in the Greek restaurant where Amy had gone unnoticed. They hadn't recognized him, but somehow he had made it onto their guest list.

Violette's seventieth. This was a party for people his age, and there would certainly be people there who remembered him. He had dressed in a tweed jacket and a red silk tie. Then he had removed the tie. Did people wear ties anymore? He did. He put the tie back on. How were people going to recognize him if he didn't dress the way he always had?

Serafina, in red-and-white satin, walked up to Hoffman as he stood in line for the elevator. Despite her dress, she was not going to the party. Just going home. "Hello, Albert," she said in a deep aromatic voice that had the quality of a whisper but could be well heard. Hoffman turned the color of Jay Mac's raspberry macaron and quickly left the building.

The number seventy played an important role for many of the people gathering for this birthday party. It made a strong and erotic impression on Art, who had thought Violette was ten years younger. Think of it. Lusting after a septuagenarian. There was something sexy about it. It was like a porn movie Art had seen about this guy who picks up an old lady and has hot and wild sex with her, except that in the movie the seventy-year-old was played by a voluptuous fifty-year-old porn star. He wanted this to be his erotic adventure. Nothing long-term, of course. He was not going to have an affair with an octogenarian.

While Art was waiting his turn for the elevator, Serafina softly slid up to him. "Going to the party with Miss Cheesecake, Artie?"

"Miss Cheesecake?"

"The one who does the girlie pictures."

Art realized that he would need to learn more New York slang before he could truly count himself assimilated. But Art thought Cato's cheesecake was truly what the party was about.

He had heard it was to be the crowning moment of an entire Roman feast that Guy had planned.

Guy was serving joyous dishes from the forlorn Apicius. He had made calf's brain sausage cooked in lovage and oregano, called isica de cerebellis. He made it with calf's brains because they were the only brains he could find. He would have preferred lamb's. He had made pheasant dumplings. Apicius had done it with peacocks. Guy thought of lying and saying his was peacock, but that might raise too many questions—and then at the first missing peacock in New York, the owners would turn up at his door. Besides, maybe Apicius had lied too.

Guy had gathered young cabbage shoots from his farm outside the city and cooked them in wine and olive oil, and he'd cooked his own fresh leeks with laurel berries. He'd made a pudding—puddings were important to classical cooking—of rose petals, red ones with the white part removed, and brains. Patina Apiciana, Apicius's specialty, was to be made with the tiny breasts of fig-pecker birds. If no fig-peckers were available—they have a summer season—Apicius suggested substituting thrush. The bird Guy was planning to serve was a mystery because there were no fig-peckers nor thrushes in the market, and Violette could not imagine him actually killing birds—especially fig-peckers because they are warblers, which he loved. Besides, it would've taken quite a few for this dish. Violette suspected he'd used quail, which could be bought cleaned in the market. But he claimed it was fig-peckers, and she was not one to reveal a secret.

The little bird breasts were cooked in a sow's stomach, an item he could get from a new organic butcher that had opened on Amsterdam (that replaced a bankrupt deli that used to have great fatty pastrami sandwiches). The new butcher sold "lean pastrami," which is as soulless as alcohol-free beer. Guy had also made a sardine loaf, and salt cod, slowly desalinated and then cooked with a honey and wine sauce. Sheep liver and lungs had been slowly stewed in sheep milk. (He may have used goat milk—he had a source.)

But what really defined the evening were the drinks, also from Apicius. By the time the last few guests gained admittance, the early arrivals were already in Apician stupors, awaiting the feast. Of course Guy had to serve Apicius's violet wine, the fine purple petals fermented with honey. Since this was a double-fermentation process done over weeks, it was far more powerful than would be expected from violet petals and honey. It was gentle enough on the first sip, but it quickly overtook you. Most people drank a glass of violet wine and, before giving it a chance to show its true character, foolishly moved on to the second Apicius specialty, absinthium Romanum.

Its recipe called for making alcohol from wormwood. In other words, absinthe, often said to be a nineteenth-century Swiss invention—but Apicius had his own recipe for it. Guy just bought the absinthe and then, as instructed, added wine and saffron. The result resembled licorice-flavored gasoline. It slowly dissolved the drinker over a period of minutes. It seemed that their joints became unfastened—first the arms and then the legs. It moved the drinker to a plateau on which their true animal nature could be discovered, whether or not they went willingly.

The guests, though slowly melting in alcohol, whispered about the cheesecake. The more they drank the more they yearned for it, but in the meantime they indulged in Guy's massacred little birds, sausages, brains, whatever they could find. The exotic food was coming but not fast enough for these alcohol-crazed appetites. The cheesecake they all had come for would be last, growing in their imagination along with their craving.

Cato's cheesecake, Sabino's really, ended up resembling a cheese-stuffed Roman villa rebuilt by modernists. The villa was mostly large cubes, but the portico had simple Doric columns. Some of the columns were tilted or broken thanks to a number of cubes that seemed to have crashed under the weight of the portico. Sabino called it an "earthquake effect." Since it was all going to go up in flames, he reasoned, it should first experience an earthquake. Then there would be angular parts that stuck out above corners of buildings or columns, providing a dramatic silhouette when engulfed in flames.

Honey was drizzled over the top, dripping off some roofs, giving a decadent, decaying look. The cheese filling, which Violette had made herself, was a rich, savory cream. But no one would ever taste it. It was like a Sabino sculpture: not for public consumption.

Guy took the cake to the garden, where he removed the kurin and kasa from the pillar before placing the masterpiece on display on top of it. Matsu, a party guest watching silently from the crowd, found this deeply offensive. But Guy had always been kind to Matsu, which intensified Matsu's lingering sense of guilt. He had wronged Guy, though Guy didn't know it—all the worse. Matsu watched Guy place the cheese-cake on the stone lantern without complaint.

. . .

She was lovely. Everyone agreed on that. "She doesn't look a day over sixty," people kept saying. "Younger than sixty." Violette, who never disappointed, was wearing a thin lavender satin shift that flowed over each curve of her body, with a few embroidered violets atop her more suggestive parts.

The New Jersey sky glowed strawberry and the inky darkness came in from Brooklyn, beautiful sadness overtaking their crowded island. People in Manhattan are certain that they are at the center of the world, but the day is always settled in New Jersey. The art world had gathered in the garden— and soon enough they were stripping, plunging into the hot tub. The shirtless director of the Metropolitan Museum of Art—a bit paunchy but with handsome square shoulders, Violette thought—came over to her and pointed downtown. They had done it. The famous spire of the Empire State Building blazed purple. Yes, the Met and its board could order this up. He leaned over and kissed Violette on the cheek—always surprising how soft a woman's cheek is—and said, "Happy birthday."

Guy spread his long arms toward the skyline as though he were praying to midtown (as all Manhattanites do sooner or later). As more violet wine and much more absinthe were consumed, a sloppy kind of casualness oozed into the gathering and ever fewer guests remained fully dressed. Violette kept her clothes on. When covering a lie it is better to be dressed. But Art kept hoping. "Cheesecake," he chuckled to himself. This was his first party at the penthouse, and it occurred to him that he might be the only one there who had never seen Violette naked. He couldn't tell if she was wearing anything under the dress. What it would be like to slide his hands along that liquid satin and around her captivating curves.

. . .

Matsu was sitting on his favorite rock by the hot tub where he and Violette used to sip chrysanthemum tea. On the next rock was hawkish Naomi. Violette could not hear what Matsu was saying to Naomi but she already knew. He was telling her how a garden is an expression of natural beauty, how it should not be a copy of nature but capture the essence of nature. Violette could lip-read key phrases. "The essence of nature." "Aware," in three careful syllables, "a-war-ee." It was the line of the man who was supposed to have "the soul of a poet."

Had she too been taken by the gift of believing?

Violette thought Naomi, who was completely absorbed in the lecture, had small breasts and sinewy arms. Maybe she could lift heavy rocks. They could lift them together. Violette wondered if she had a red hawk's tail too, but it looked as though she had nothing back there at all.

Violette understood what was happening. She had not often had this feeling, this greasy, flowing ache of jealousy. The last time might've been when she first saw beneath Sister Mary's robes. Art noticed it too. *So Violette didn't always keep her marriage vows.* Maybe none of these people did. He could see that she had been involved with that Japanese guy . . . and maybe with some others here. Art examined the crowd, trying to pick out Violette's lovers. Then, really by chance, he found himself standing next to her looking out at the skyline.

"Some view," he said, which was the only thing to say in that situation.

"Yes," she said patiently, "but it is getting worse. They keep building things. We're getting out."

"Really?" he said in his real estate voice.

"Yes, Guy wants to live on the farm."

"And you?"

"Me too."

Art saw his opening. "Won't you miss having a place here? I could get you a nice apartment. A nice pied-à-terre for spending time in the city. I'm renting to this crazy lady with a big apartment. She has a trapeze and a glass sculpture hanging from the ceiling. I'm trying to get rid of her. I could let you have the place for a nice price."

"I bet it's a nice price now."

"Well, more than she was paying. She was robbing me. But I can give you a good price. Better than market."

"I'll have to think about it." And she fell into a silence that Art could see was the end of the conversation. But Art could also see that at this gathering, you could get away with anything. He put his hands on either side of her waist and slid them down—the satin felt so good—on to her hips. "Look," he said, "why don't we take off our clothes like everyone else and hit the hot tub." He was feeling confident. He had a good body. Not as good as that Japanese guy. But a lot better than most of the men he saw here. And maybe she'd slept with some of them too? They were all sleeping with each other. That's what this crowd did. And she was not removing his hands. He guessed it would only take a single smooth gesture to drop the slip.

"I don't think so," she said with a smile that showed that she was genuinely amused. And she walked away.

. . .

It was time.

Guy heated a pan of Roman absinthe and held a lit match to it. *Woof*, it made the sound of a monster inhaling. The pan exploded in a bright blue flame that he poured over the Roman cheesecake to please the gods.

"Happy birthday, Violette," Guy said, and the guests repeated it, some unfortunately saying, "Happy seventieth." *Who says that*, thought Violette. But after no more than a few seconds, the blue fire was gone and Cato's cheesecake reappeared, unchanged. Guy tried to light it again with the same result.

Sabino brought over a small handheld blowtorch. The torch burned a hole through the façade, like a new window for the villa. But the cheesecake wouldn't light. Guy threw his hands up like he was tossing them away. "You can't eat it. You can't burn it. What the hell." It was as though he was finally grasping the fall of the Roman Empire.

The fickle crowd had lost interest in the main event. Sipping exotic Roman cocktails, nibbling exotic Roman brains, they had all become weirdly omnivorous. Historians say this happened in first-century imperial Rome too, Apicius's time. They started eating the garden—a leaf here, a blossom there. The garden was delicious.

A man they called Pink Hammy Ross fell into the amaranth. He looked like a pig at lunchtime, and no one is happier than a lunching pig. A modern art curator began eating orchids; a gallery owner was munching on chrysanthemums. Diane Davis, the prima ballerina who, without a tutu, had almost no visible body at all, descended to all fours, landing as softly as a wasp on a flower petal, and began grazing on the leaves and little blue flowers of the buddleia beloved by the butterflies. She stuck her pursed lips out from her narrow face like a pollinating proboscis.

Paulo Cenci, the tall, lean sculptor, resembling a hungry giraffe, reached up and plucked the green top leaves of Matsu's mochi tree with his mouth. Everyone called Paulo "Giacometti," not because his abstract metal work resembled the earlier master's, but because Paulo himself looked like one of his sculptures.

Harold Demmings, whose biography of Gauguin everyone was talking about—what is more valuable than an art book with gossip—dropped to his hands and knees to join the delicate Diane, grazing on the fine buddleia, although it was not difficult to see that he would rather have been sampling the ballerina. Violette decided that Harold looked more natural on all fours than he had ever looked standing on his feet.

Several people sampled the tempting little flowers of the white alder bush, a good plant to feed on because the evergreen was indestructible and the little white blossoms came out all year long. Better that than the seasonal reddish *Calluna* heather. Camellia, behind it, had been planted in a far corner because it was fussy and could not bear a limey soil. As the crowds flowed, an occasional foot or naked thigh, a leg, an arm could be briefly seen behind that glossy thick evergreen. Behind the buckthorn, whose delectable orange berries were being completely ignored, was another couple. A groan, a sigh could be heard. A few anonymous people should always be making love in the background of a successful soirée. Only Harold uttered what any number of them might have been thinking. "Absinthe makes the heart grow fonder."

Matsu, seeing his garden being eaten (which he thought might not be an unjust fate for a garden), got dressed and left without even trying to conceal from Violette that he was taking a certain hawk with him. Harold left with Diane. One by one, or two by two, they all left. Some still had a telltale leaf or flower petal hanging on a lip. Some had green teeth. What would the doorman think? Art had retreated to Serafina on the fourth floor, who joked that she would give him "a fair market price."

By daybreak, Guy and Violette were alone except for the anonymous couple asleep behind the heather and the dark shiny curtain of camellia bush—and Hammy Ross, who had faded in the amaranth after mostly clearing the bed, a last leaf hanging from the side of his mouth as he slept a sated porcine slumber.

· · ·

The fresh day's brilliant new rays shot in sideways from Brooklyn, lit up the faces of tall buildings, and made Manhattan look like a jeweler had carved it from gold. A black-and-yellow great spangled fritillary rested on Guy's shoulder, reminding Violette that she had seen a butterfly briefly perch on Art's bald shiny pate the previous night. It had looked comic and she had laughed, though she could see that he did not know why. But it had suggested to her that this man must have deeper qualities than she'd thought. You can trust the judgment of butterflies.

"Look at that," said Guy. "Four new buildings. I wonder when they'll have us boxed in. Time goes quickly."

"It could be slower than we know." Violette looked around. "The garden looks as though goats ate it," she said.

Guy smiled. "Sometimes you have to feed the goats."

"Did Cato say that?" Violette asked.

"Cato," Guy said. "What did he know? What was he thinking with that goddamned cheesecake?"

11

Cato and the Luftmensch

Fate had ignored the destiny of Lazarus Vanderthal's wealthy name, and he didn't care anymore. He had given up entirely on caring. He had never even been almost rich. He had never wanted to be mentioned in *Fortune* magazine, and he increasingly hoped never to be mentioned at all.

His mother, in the lunchroom of P.S. 84, always pushed him to "do better." He had been confident that he would, especially since his father had not set an especially high bar. When he asked why he was named Lazarus, she answered, "Because your father was a luftmensch." That was all she would say on the subject. She could not even explain the word. "A luftmensch is a luftmensch," she clarified, adding, "it's a luftmensch."

At the age of fourteen, Lazarus was determined to launch his career. Having grown up loving Hungarian treats, he decided to become a baker and got a job making croissants on Seventy-Second Street. A croissant maker never stops moving, mixing and rolling and folding and rolling and placing on sheets and baking and mixing more while the previous batch is rising and baking—and if Lazarus ever had a moment's break, it needed to be used to sweep the flour from the floor.

At the end of the day he longed to collapse on a couch and enjoy not moving. But it was a beginning—he was launching a career. His croissants were good. He was ready to move up to something more important—cheesecake had been suggested—when the bakery's rent was raised and it was forced to close. He tried the bakery down the street but found that they were closing too. He went over to Columbus Avenue to a small café, where soon he was making not only a marble cheesecake but a Dobos torte, artfully arranging the caramel wedges on top. He was becoming a skilled baker. By the time the Gap bought them out, he had the skill to go elsewhere, up to Grossinger's on West Eighty-Eighth Street, where they even promised to train him to make their famous praline ice cream cake.

But soon they were closed too. He thought he had learned a useful skill, but there was nowhere to use it. He even went to the Krispy Kreme donut shop that had taken over the storefront of the old Austrian Jewish bakery where he had started out making croissants. But Krispy Kreme wasn't hiring bakers. *There must still be bakers in Little Italy,* he thought. *They must be able to use a cheesecake maker.* Little Italy was the reverse of the Upper West Side, where the neighborhood was expanding and the bakeries vanishing. In Little Italy, the neighborhood had been shrinking for decades, pressed against Chinatown to the east, but the bakeries were surviving. The rumor was that the Sicilians looked after their own, so Lazarus the Luft-mensch headed downtown using the name Johnny Palermo. He used a few Italian words, and some of the gruff business owners spoke it back to him. He didn't realize that their words were Sicilian, not Italian. They easily detected that his was a phony name: he must be an Italian trying to pose as a Sicil-ian. It didn't matter. They had no job openings.

Lazarus came to understand that the problem was not that he was a baker but that he was a luftmensch. Would anyone hire a luftmensch? (Though he still did not know what that meant.) He wondered if he could ever stop being one. He thought that it had something to do with not being grounded. Being grounded? He did not really know what that meant either.

For a time he was a busboy. Then a waiter. Sometimes tips were good, but he knew he had to save in good times for bad. Then he found a job as "a market researcher." Now *there* was a job that was grounded. It had a future. Though not a huge amount more money, the pay was steady—and since the job sounded important, it might lead to a job that really was. It had a white-collar feel to it. There were a dozen market researchers, working in a room for a pollster. It turned out that if you asked a few thousand people the same question they would only have four different responses. There were a few with something either original or idiotic. These answers were thrown away in a column titled "None of the above." His job was to find the four common responses and fit as many answers as possible into one of these categories. If more than five percent were "none of the above," you had done it wrong. But you could almost always fit most answers into one of four responses.

Lazarus had felt like his life was beginning to take shape. He left his mother's small apartment and was able to rent a studio in a doorman building on West Eighty-Sixth Street. He liked the respect that was paid to him by the uniformed building staff. It confirmed that his status had improved. He furnished the apartment with serviceable old pieces from a store on Columbus that had endless affordable choices, some sturdier than others. He even asked a neighbor, Marsha Weber, on a date. Marsha was skilled at choosing clothing that showed off an ample body but she also had a warm smile—an irresistible combination. They would find something to talk about.

He really couldn't afford what people in this building considered a date. She had a two-bedroom apartment. She confessed it was rent stabilized and she was probably not spending much more than he was paying for his studio. Still, single women with two-bedroom apartments had expectations. He might have invited her to a movie but then he would have been expected to take her somewhere afterward, so he decided going straight to the afterward: asking her to a dinner would be better.

He found an affordable little Italian place.

Early in the evening he was already wishing it would be over. She probably was too. She had a job but he could not understand what she did. She couldn't understand his job either. He thought she mustn't like the way he was obviously trying to spend as little money as possible. Tap water. Only a small salad for him. He said that he was a vegetarian. Maybe she didn't like vegetarians. Actually, he didn't either. He was poor and she could tell and she didn't like him being poor and he didn't like her not liking him being poor. They got back to the building as soon as they could and ended the evening in the lobby. He headed up later to avoid the awkward elevator ride. It ended with a squeezeless handshake.

They would sometimes see each other in the lobby or on the street and once even in a long silent elevator ride. He would smile but there was no infrastructure behind it to hold the smile in place. No question of a date number two. Ever.

Eventually he was to learn that renting his apartment had been a mistake anyway. His landlord could keep raising the rent, making him increasingly desperate to pay for it. Then in 1990 his mother died. Had he continued to live with her, he would have been able to keep her rent-stabilized apartment with very low rent. But he had lost his claim.

Strange things were happening in his building. The lobby became air-conditioned. He could hear construction work in the apartments. It was going co-op. He was offered a bargain "insider's price," but he didn't have that money either. If he had had "a little insider money," he wondered years later, would his life have turned out differently? He struggled to pay his rent, which was still low but ever rising. Then he lost his market research job. The company closed. Computers replaced market researchers. He had been better off as a busboy—they could never be computerized. He found a job in a store, then in a restaurant. Then he drove a taxi, but the salary was low and the tips were bad. As a beginner, he was forced to take the weekend shift and often was stuck in a rut between Bloomingdale's and the Upper East Side. He needed a few airport trips. He lost the taxi job too. Between jobs there was his unemployment benefit, which he got by standing in a long line downtown once a week. The jobs had not paid well when he had them, so the unemployment compensation—only a percentage of his earnings—was not much. Sometimes he would supplement his budget by shoplifting food from supermarkets. It was wonderful, the way food was packed in flat packages that were easy to hide in a sweater or jacket.

He tried to spend as little as possible so he would be able to make rent. He had to pay his rent. One day he found that he couldn't come up with the money—and then this continued for months. In time he learned that the climb upward is jagged and uneven but the trip down is a swift and fluid slide. He could not find another job and he was tired of looking. Tired of struggling. Tired of jobs so worthless a computer wouldn't even bother to take them over. He had been doing this for fifteen years. He was not the kind of tired that could be fixed by going to bed and sleeping. It was the kind that made him sit down and give up. He was just tired of trying.

He didn't pay rent for three months. Four? Five? He lost track. But the landlord was keeping track, and he was evicted. Lazarus left his few possessions behind. All he kept was a warm coat and a cup labeled BRADEN & WHITE MARKET RESEARCH when he moved to the street.

A relief. The struggle was over. There was a shelter only a block away, but shelters had rules. The whole point of the street was to escape rules. He chose a suitable stretch of sidewalk— *were there rules for this?*—but a man he knew as Mr. Katz, Art, told him he was squatting in front of his building and couldn't stay. Lazarus recognized him from the diner. "Mr. Katz, it's Lazarus. I used to be a regular at the diner." Mr. Katz didn't care and told him to move.

Lazarus moved to a comfortable spot on the corner of West Eighty-Sixth and Columbus, propped against the Plexiglas bus stop shelter. The stops had recently been redesigned to make the streets look better, also to have no benches for homeless people to sleep on. But you could lean against them on the outside. He put out the coffee cup. Sometimes passersby would drop in a coin or two, or even a dollar or two. He didn't care. He had no more bills to pay. He was free to sit and think. He enjoyed the early morning when people were just emerging from their apartments, mostly to walk their dogs. He enjoyed watching chubby Rosita slapping certain windshields with parking tickets because they were on the wrong side of the street for the day. That was what life was like. Some people always knew where to be on which day. Others never knew. Lazarus wondered if that was what a luftmensch was—someone who never knows.

A few days after he had settled on the street, on trash day, he saw his old furniture on the curb. Apartment dwellers, people with homes, were going through the trash looking for a find. A young couple he recognized from his building had selected the table he had bought for very little on Columbus Avenue. They were tapping it to see if it was solid. But they missed the weak leg. Lazarus wondered if he should tell them, but they walked off with it looking pleased.

At first he thought it would be embarrassing to be homeless in his old neighborhood. Mr. Katz had not received him well. He had no more relatives around, but there were people he had known all his life. Joey De Falco, who owned the bodega on Columbus, and Tommy Mateo, who grew up with him and was now a doorman on Eighty-Sixth Street. Tommy walked by Lazarus every day but only saw a homeless person. The staff at his old building didn't recognize him either. Or they didn't acknowledge him, anyway. Neither did Hoffman, the sour-faced man who had once lived next door and had never said hello. He was still sour-faced and still didn't say hello. He often saw Marsha Weber and he would give her the same flaccid smile he had used before, but she didn't recognize it. Once, in a perverse mood, he asked her for a dollar. Still no recognition. Also no dollar.

A nice older woman dressed in black who had once invited him to a huge party in her apartment walked right up to him, with a face full of sympathy but not much eye contact, and handed him two neatly folded dollar bills, like a packet she had prepared to give out to homeless people. She didn't recognize him either. A beautiful blonde woman, who he had once been told was a famous model, handed him a five-dollar bill and a smile. It was more than a five-dollar smile. He was grateful. It turned out that this neighborhood was full of money. Without ever asking, some days his market research cup had more money stuffed in it than he'd have made in a day of busboy tips. For the most part, though, people from his building, whom he had once greeted every day, walked right by him.

One sunny afternoon Ruth Arnstein pushed, clunked, and dragged her walker right up to him. He recognized her from the building next door. She was the building terror, always raising one issue or another and trying to enlist the support of other tenants in her campaigns. She seemed to recognize him. Lazarus braced himself. Ruth Arnstein was going to try to help him, give him health advice, order him to a shelter, tell him how to get money or food.

But all she did was hand him a long knit red scarf. "Here," she said. "Stay warm, kiddo. You don't want to get pneumonia or something." Ruth was adapting to walker life. She had gotten herself one with a basket to replace her Zabar's bag. The basket held Band-Aids, candy for children, bread for birds, treats for dogs, dollar bills for beggars, and even a spare scarf.

Lazarus stared after her and wondered, *So is that a luftmensch?*

He didn't care much about money anymore. He didn't have a lot to spend it on. It was more important that the neighborhood was full of food. It must have been the most wasteful neighborhood in New York. People who have money are used to throwing it away.

Expensive restaurants like Mykonos threw out lamb and fish and cheese. Lazarus supposed they served too much food to customers who couldn't eat it all. It was too bad that the bakeries were gone or there would have been tortas, croissants, and cheesecake, day-old but still good. Quality bakeries have a lot to throw out at the end of the day. He used to live on yesterday's croissants.

One day Lazarus was working a trash bin and found the remains of a lamb shank. While his thoughts wandered to the wastefulness of the rich, another hungry man working the same trash bin grabbed the shank from him. Lazarus knew him. He was the one they called "Old Mr. Boston." Old Mr. Boston was younger than he was—and he was not from Boston, either. His name was Earl and he had grown up in the neighborhood. Maybe someone had seen him drinking from a bottle of Old Mr. Boston. He now had rust-colored, weathered skin, a kinky beard that looked like a cloud of dark smoke, and hair that fell over his face in a great long mop—but it was certainly Earl. Everyone had said he was a genius. He had gone to MIT at age seventeen, so in a sense he was from Boston. Everyone knew that Earl the genius was at MIT, then that he was rumored to have a big secret job for NASA. And then no more was heard about him. When he swiped Lazarus's lamb shank, which still had some meat on it, Lazarus let him have it. You can't compete with a genius.

Earl seldom spoke, though Lazarus did once hear him explain to a policeman that he remained barefoot because "they use your shoes to control you" and politely warned the uniformed man against wearing them.

There were many other places to find food—other garbage cans and street corners. Late on busy nights there were boxes of pizza, only half the slices taken, sitting on the sidewalk, along with half-eaten roasted chickens, leftover sandwich halves. Once he even found a barely eaten chocolate cake. Overbaked cake, sure, but good buttercream. It wasn't even stale. A birthday gone wrong?

Lazarus realized that, after all the time he had spent shoplifting food while living in his apartment, he could've just been looking through the bags in the hallway where his neighbors left out their trash. Sometimes, especially at dawn—a welcome time because nights are long on the street—before the doormen started cleaning, the sidewalks were scattered with discarded food. Meat and rice dishes in white Styrofoam trays. Or a partially drunk beer? Or a half-full can of Coke? Most people, it seemed, didn't finish. Lazarus wondered if that was why there were so many divorces. Just popped into his head. Could that be right? He would have to think about it.

On the street, Lazarus learned that you had to examine everything before the doormen came out, spraying the sidewalks with their hoses. By nine o'clock the world was wet and clean. They would even slather white gunk on the brass awning poles to rub them until they gleamed. On certain days, building staff would pile black bags along the curbs for the garbage trucks. These were the important days to Lazarus, bigger than a sale at Bloomingdale's to the people leaving the food in the first place. The garbage men were willing to let the homeless help themselves as long as they weren't sloppy, and most of them put whatever they didn't want back in the bags. The recycling bags full of bottles and cans also often held items of interest. Many liquor bottles had two or three shots left at the bottom.

Lazarus found a bottle marked ABSINTHE. He didn't know what that was, but it was marked a formidable 140 proof. About a quarter of the bottle was still there. He slipped it into his coat. That alone would have been a good morning. But then he found something extraordinary in the garbage.

He wasn't sure what it was—some kind of model of a monument or fancy building. He didn't even know if it was edible. He broke off a pillar and tried to eat it. It was crunchy. It tasted like grain, maybe whole wheat. And some of it had sticky sweet stuff on it. He ate an entire pillar and he felt good. This food was dense and filling. Then he realized that, like those Hostess cakes he loved as a child, it had a surprise inside. It was filled with cheese, a smooth cheese filling. This was someone's cheesecake. What extraordinary baker, still in the neighborhood, had made this!

Old Mr. Boston observed Lazarus from a slight distance. He was always that way—keeping a slight distance. That was why it had surprised Lazarus when he grabbed the lamb shank, but even geniuses can be driven by hunger. If he was so brilliant, Lazarus wanted his opinion on this architectural spectacle. He showed the cake to Old Mr. Boston.

"What do you think it is?"

Old Mr. Boston had only the briefest hesitation. "The architecture is Roman. Pre-Empire. Republic, I should think." He broke off a piece and crunched and swallowed it. Then he took another piece. He started for a third, but Lazarus blocked his hand. "So what is it?"

"Tastes like an ancient recipe. Maybe an ancient grain." He began reciting something in Latin and was still going on when Lazarus abandoned him. He might go on that way for days. You never knew with Old Mr. Boston.

This sculpture was food for a week, an entire week in which he didn't have to do any more hunting—not until the next trash day. It reminded him of the time he had managed to shove five rib-eye steaks in his sweater to bring home from the supermarket. That had been an easy week, but this one would be even better because he had no rent to worry about. He found a large green plastic bag promising the best prices on men's wear. He put his prize inside and went home to his bus stop corner to relax. He sat down with his back against the Plexiglas and felt good. He thought about the Romans and closed his eyes to block out the legs walking by, taking three hard pulls from the absinthe bottle. A slow kind of heat took over his body and rocked him to sleep.

. . .

The Fucker was making his way up Columbus. Everyone called him that because that was what he said to everyone. As he walked up or down the street, taking strides like a politician running for office, he would try to make eye contact with anyone he could. This was not as easy as it sounded because New Yorkers generally avoid eye contact with homeless people, strangers, anyone you could not be sure of. People would turn their heads or stare down as though their feet had invented a new kind of step. Anything to avoid his wild-eyed stare. But at the same time, they couldn't help but glance at the man making himself look as wild and dangerous as possible. Only a few would get caught.

Then he would say to the trapped passerby, "Fuck you!" He had the gift of clarity. Sometimes he would walk up and shout, "Shut the fuck up!" He regarded that as his more poetic testimonial. Either way, people were afraid of him. He loved that. "Just think of it," he would tell himself, because he had no one else to whom he could tell it. "Here I am. Absolutely nobody. Even toward the bottom of the nobody list. And yet all the rich people of New York live in terror of me. I petrify them. Isn't that something great? Isn't life fantastic? Fuck them! Fuck all of you! Fuck you!"

He really was tough, though. One night a raccoon walked up to him and he landed a right cross-hook on its head, stunning the animal and knocking it over before it ran away. "Fuck you too," he called after it.

Sometimes passersby would call the police. But the police knew him. They would talk to him for a few minutes, during which he would always be softspoken and polite. Then as they walked away, he would shout, "Fuck you too!" They expected it, and waved back.

The Fucker rounded Eighty-Sixth Street. There was the one they called Lazarus, sound asleep, clutching something in a green plastic bag. The Fucker wouldn't have thought anything of the bag if Lazarus hadn't been clutching it so tightly. *It must be something good.* The Fucker leaned down and, with a sweeping motion of his right arm, grabbed the bag and hurried off. Art, happening to pass by on his way to the restaurant, saw that the Fucker had robbed a sleeping man. He started to say something, but the Fucker just said, "Fuck you!" Art Katz was not going to get into a fight with a homeless man—and especially not with one who was rumored to have punched out a raccoon.

When Lazarus woke up, he realized his green plastic bag was gone even before he opened his eyes. He sighed, not only because it was gone but because he knew who had taken it. A week or two earlier—he was not sure how long ago, two garbage days at least—his market research mug had vanished while he was sleeping. He later saw it on the Fucker's blanket. He could have taken it back, but he hadn't moved to the streets to continue caring about material possessions. Food, however, was different from possessions, and it was becoming clear that life on the street wasn't completely free. A man like the Fucker would keep preying on you until you stopped him. Just like a landlord. Street life was not all that different.

The Fucker lived on a blanket on the church steps on Amsterdam. It was an old brownstone church, and developers were trying to tear it down to build apartments. Neighborhood committees had posted signs denouncing the project. When Lazarus got there, he found the Fucker admiring his cheese-filled building.

"Hey! That's mine! I want it back!" Lazarus hadn't used an aggressive voice, or made a demand, in so long that his voice cracked and squeaked with anger.

"Fuck you!" The predictable response.

Desperate and having no more faith in the power of his voice, Lazarus ran over to the Fucker and the cheese-filled building. Even as he ran, he wasn't sure it was the right thing to do. The Fucker was the type who might've carried a knife. Some of them did. Street people were killed fairly often. If a homeless person wanted to kill another homeless person, they could. No one would care, so the police didn't have to care either as long as it didn't happen too often. They'd just pick up the corpse without asking questions.

Lazarus and the Fucker weren't exactly fighting, but they were still pulling and grabbing to gain possession of the cheese-filled building when a loud whooshing sound came from behind them, like when the garbage men hoist the trash bags into their trucks to be ground up.

Was it a gun?

They both turned, almost dropping their prize. Coming toward them was a killer monster from another world. Its eyes were ebonized fire, hunter's eyes with meat in their sights. A beak like the razor-sharp curved sword of a medieval Saracen about to decapitate an enemy. The monster was enlarged by huge flapping wings, powerful appendages that looked ready to slap away anything in its path. It hovered over the two men, seeming to know this would make them shrink away and back off. It descended, deadly claws coming down like the landing gear of an airplane. These were clearly weapons. The claws grabbed the cheese-filled building and lifted it into the air. Then the red hawk flew with strength and grace, high above the street, carrying its prize to its home in a nest above West Eighty-Fifth Street.

Lazarus and the Fucker sat down on the blanket and thought. What was this creature and why did she want the cheese-filled building? Did it mean something to her? Was this a beast who just took to the air with whatever she liked? Was that what was meant by a luftmensch! Lazarus spent most of the day contemplating but found no answers to his questions.

12

Art Discovers Art

Crazy Mrs. Landau, with her ghostlike white hair and her house full of junk, gave Art an idea. To give Mykonos just the right tone, the restaurant needed art on the walls. Mrs. Landau's walls were covered with it. What was she going to do with it all when she was moved? Right now, all they had in the restaurant was a framed photo of their Cato's cheesecake taken by a well-known food photographer (or at least Art said she was well-known), for which they'd paid plenty.

Crazy Mrs. Landau owned five woodcuts of desserts that would be perfect for the restaurant. "How much do you want for them?"

"A year at your new fair market rent," Mimi replied.

Art hesitated, not only because this was an enormous price but also because Mimi was set to move out and he wanted her gone as soon as possible. "Seems like a lot," Art said, "for woodcuts from an unknown artist."

"He is not unknown. Only his whereabouts are unknown."

"Still seems like a lot."

"Seems like a lot for a year's rent."

"It's the market. I can easily get it."

In the end they settled on just one for sixteen thousand dollars. She hated to give one up, especially to him, but she was going to have to find another place to live and she needed the money. Still, sixteen thousand dollars seemed an outrageous price for a woodcut. You could find a better deal for a Rembrandt. But since Lewiston St. Jean had mysteriously disappeared and left only a few works behind, people would pay for them. An unfair price, but perhaps a "fair market price."

For Art, the price confirmed the value. He always believed that. The more he charged for apartments, the more they were worth. At sixteen thousand dollars, this was an important piece of art. When he proudly hung the woodcut in the dining room of the Mykonos, Adara and Niki were not impressed.

"It's not even a dessert that we sell," Adara argued.

"It's a famous artist," Art countered.

"That's what you said about this," said Adara, pointing to the bright color photograph of Cato's cheesecake. Adara wanted to decorate with pictures of her favorite goats, especially a black-and-white head shot of Cassandra, a loving nanny goat with shyly drooping ears and a sweet penetrating gaze. Niki wanted to hang his favorite picture of Adara, also black-and-white, in which she was feeding Cassandra's kid with a baby milk bottle.

. . .

Now that crazy Mrs. Landau had agreed to leave the apartment, Art was patient with her. It would take time to move all her belongings. Besides, Guy and Violette were gone and Art saw no sign of them. He was expecting Violette but she did not appear.

Art had arranged to view their old apartment under the guise that he was considering buying it, but he really wanted to confirm that they had left. The sculptures, lanterns, bridge, even the rocks were gone from the garden, and the greenery was unkempt, like morning hair after a bad night. The large apartment was completely empty, now looking even larger. Some blue paint was splattered on the floor in one corner. In another there was a crushed tube of vermillion oil paint, a small empty bottle of cold-pressed linseed oil, and a palette knife with the handle broken off. A scrap of paper with a poem in Latin that Art couldn't read—something about dinner. There was also a single old-fashioned white-and-black sneaker and an empty box of Uncle Tetsu Japanese cheesecake. That was all that was left of them.

. . .

When the summer flowers were gone and the tree planters along West Eighty-Sixth Street were replanted with begonias for the fall, Violette walked into Mykonos and asked for Art. She wore nothing as overwhelming as her purple satin birthday slip but she looked refreshed, like the first breeze of fall, in a beige linen dress cinched at the waist, making the skirt flare over stockinged legs that gave off a slightly electric hiss as she moved. That subtle sound, one most people would not even hear, thrilled Art.

"How's life on the farm?"

"Life on the farm is beautiful and peaceful."

"Not like here."

"No. Manhattan used to be beautiful but now there are too many skinny new buildings cluttering the sky. My husband lives to look at beauty. If something doesn't look beautiful anymore, he doesn't want to look at it."

Could she be talking about herself? Was this Guy a complete fool? Or was this Violette expressing an anti–real estate attitude, which would not be a good signal for him? But then she said something he'd been hoping to hear.

"But I've been thinking, I would like a place to stay here from time to time. As you said, a pied-à-terre."

To Art, there was a certain heat, something sexy and suggestive about the way she said "pied-à-terre." French was the language of eroticism. Maybe "pied" reminded him of how sexy her long feet were. He had seen her barefoot at the birthday party and could never forget it. But Art found something sexy and suggestive in everything Violette said—even the way she ordered a root beer float. He had never recovered from the sight of her sucking on the straw, either.

"Pied-à-terre" was a phrase that meant different things to different people. Art knew what *he* meant, and he could only hope she had the same meaning. He knew a Jewish landlord on the East Side, one of the old building owners who had sold off some but still owned quite a few. He had told Art that the son of his real estate agency's founder had met a twenty-four-year-old who found him "devastating." Mort gave the young woman a penthouse, a pied-à-terre for the two of them that his wife didn't need to know about. When

Art heard this story, he imagined that it must be going on all over the city—a perk of owning Manhattan real estate.

Art thought giving Violette the apartment rent-free would be taking things too far. Certainly she would be insulted by the suggestion. He would just offer her a good price, and she'd be able to see that he was making money. He thought that was part of his charm.

. . .

Art went to the gift shop of the Metropolitan Museum and bought a quality canvas reproduction of *Violette in Moonlight* in a gilded wooden frame. He eagerly unwrapped it on a table in Mykonos while Adara and Niki watched with a sense of impending doom. With his arms spread wide, Art held out the framed picture as he turned, searching the walls for the right spot. Then he walked over to the large black-and-white goat photo.

"No. Not Cassandra."

Without even looking at Adara, Art explained that they had two other "goat pics": the photo of her feeding the kid and now a somewhat comical group goat picture that, of course, included Cassandra. "This is a restaurant of the classics. It can't just have livestock on the walls. We need art."

Silently, unhappily, the family could see Art's point. Art was good at these things. He knew what he was doing. He'd made them rich, though more from his real estate ventures than from the restaurant.

Art looked at his painting and the large cheesecake photo and he thought "two kinds of cheesecake," but he kept this joke to himself and hoped that most people would have more artsy thoughts.

. . .

Saul Putz came in to talk to Adara about a television special he was thinking of producing on Cato's cheesecake. He found her in one of the restaurant's slow business lunches. Art's idea for a less expensive business lunch special had not been a success; the wealthy tenants renting their apartments tended to work and lunch downtown. Today only two other tables were occupied—one by an actual pair of businessmen in suits, and the other by Linda.

Saul had tried to get Guy to speak on record about his rendition of the cheesecake, but Guy had become a recluse on a farm. Saul was able to talk to Sabino Begotxu about building the cheesecake for Violette's birthday, but Sabino's description of how he fashioned a semi-edible cheesecake that failed to burn up was not tempting fare for food television. Sabino didn't really want to be on television.

But when Saul approached Mykonos, Art immediately saw the possibilities. He told Saul that the cheesecake had been developed and was still being made by Adara. Art was certain that Adara would look as good on camera as she did in real life. Niki agreed. She had the makings of a television food star. Saul would have to see her on camera. They wanted him to meet her in her kitchen in Queens. It would be great TV. There were two problems.

One: Saul did not go to Queens. If something had to be done in Queens he would send someone else. He would go to Brooklyn or possibly the Bronx, but Saul did not do Queens.

Two: It did not matter if it was great television because Saul had no intention of actually producing a television special about Cato's cheesecake. He was only gathering information for Masha's bat mitzvah.

So there Saul was, interviewing Adara in a quiet corner of Mykonos during a quiet business lunch, trying like a secret agent to extract information. Linda was at the next table listening to every word, enjoying the veal special and a glass of Provençal rosé. She had a number of good ideas for television specials and had long wanted to sit down with Saul Putz just as Adara was doing now. How had Adara managed it? What was the right way to pitch him? Linda was listening. Trying to contribute, she tossed one of her classic conversation stoppers: "Wasn't Cato a fascist?"

Saul looked up at the large color photo of the cheesecake as though he hadn't seen it before. ". . . Is that a Grace Harrigan?" he asked.

Pleased, Art walked over. "Yes, it is." Pointing to the woodcut next to it, he added, "And did you see this? It's a Louis St. Jean."

"I don't know him," said Saul, who probably wouldn't have even had Art gotten the name right. This confirmed Art's fears about the purchase.

"He's from Barbados or something like that," Art argued weakly.

"But that's not a cheesecake," said Linda, chiming in. "A cake or torta or something."

"Oh, and there's Violette," said Saul. "Beautiful painting." Art wondered if that was all he could see. He didn't think straitlaced Saul had the same thoughts he had. But he dreaded Linda, who he was sure in a moment would say something like, "Oh yeah, the one with the root beer."

Niki, trying to rescue the moment and keep the TV man focused on his beautiful wife, pointed to the photo of Adara feeding the kid. "That's my favorite picture of Adara," he said.

"Which one is Adara?" asked Linda, who didn't know the Katz family.

13

Alone in Her Lair

Mimi placed the cold six-pack of cider on the floor and sat down next to it. This was the year you were supposed to drink hard cider instead of beer. There was no explaining these things. She selected a bottle and twisted the cap off, then took a long pull, downing about a third. It was not unlike beer—the same size bubbles, a different kind of tartness, the same alcohol. But fruit and grain would never be the same. She took two more deep pulls and opened a second bottle.

She looked around the room. This was she. All of it. When it was gone, she would no longer exist. She was saying farewell to herself. Of course, by the third bottle she was thinking more practically about how she was going to dispose of it all. How do you pack up a grand piano or a hanging glass sculpture?

She stood up, walked to the highly polished piano, and started Chopin's first Ballade in G minor, a sad, rich key signature. The piece was supposed to express Chopin's yearning for faraway Poland. Someday, Mimi thought, almost with a smile, she would write a ballade to her vanished apartment. Mid-phrase she stood up and walked to her pinball machine. She snapped the lever and the ball flew, bounced off a few flippers, and disappeared.

She was about to shoot out a second ball when she had a better idea. She walked over to the trapeze, leapt up, grabbed the bar with both hands, and swung back and forth a few times until she had the momentum to flip up and stand on her hands. She grabbed the side ropes with her ankles and slid down until she was hanging by her feet. She took broad swings, her shock of hair unfurling like a white flag, sweeping along the floor as she swung. After a few minutes of ever more vigorous upside-down arcs, she swung around until she was standing on the trapeze bar. She took a deep bow to the audience that wasn't there. Then she decided that while she still had a great kitchen she would make a truly great cheesecake. After all, this was West Eighty-Sixth Street.

14

The Arnold Reuben of the Twenty-First Century

"Frankly, I walked out of there thinking, 'Where's the ganache?'"

That was Sarah's verdict on Cato's cheesecake at Mykonos. Saul and Masha gritted their teeth.

She was on the ganache again. Sarah was monothematic. Once she got stuck on something she would keep repeating her argument, often in one-word form. When they decided to buy a car, she declared she wanted a Prius. She didn't argue for it. She expressed no preference for the new idea of hybrid cars, nor a concern about burning fossil fuels. No one had ever heard her discuss climate change. She never even specified which model she preferred, although when pressed once by Masha, she responded that she would prefer a red one. But at every conversation she would simply say "Prius" and eventually they bought a Prius, probably one of the first on the Upper West Side. Now they would eat ganache.

"Listen, Masha," Saul argued. "This is the oldest known recipe in the world. No one else will have it. Something unique and special"—the Prius argument—"praised by the *New York Times*."

Dad was talking Masha's language and he knew it. But then Mom added, "Cato, schmato, put in some ganache or it will be boring. Everybody likes ganache. Don't you love it, Masha?"

Yes, she loved it. She wasn't sure what it was, but it was chocolate and it was fattening, so what more was there? She happened to know that Rachel Rabbinowitz's one weakness, her Achilles' heel, as they might say over at Mykonos, was chocolate. Masha had seen it. On two separate occasions she'd seen Rachel devouring a bag of M&Ms in a corner like a retriever with a stolen hamburger.

The first rule of the School of American Ballet was not to take warm-up stretches seriously or to arch your back or to extend your neck. The first rule was that you were not, under any circumstance, to eat food. The first sign of a belly or a breast or having an upper arm thicker than your forearm, and you were out. Dancers were expected to maintain the body of an eel. Masha knew that when Diane Davis graced her event, all her parents' friends would be whispering, "Poor thing. She needs to eat something." That was the look. Looked good under lights in a tutu.

With her mother's help, Masha thought she could destroy Rachel with ganache. It would be her weapon. But Saul confessed that though he'd tried, he could not get Adara to reveal her secret recipe, not even for television—especially not for television.

"Well, I'll reveal a secret," said Sarah. "It would be a lot better with some ganache."

In any case, Saul was convinced that they had to have the cheesecake. He was impressed with the way the Katsikases got so much attention for it. He thought he would strengthen the argument with his rabbinical voice and gestures.

"The haftarah is from the Book of Samuel."

Masha was already rolling her eyes, but Saul pressed on.

"David's brothers were fighting the Philistines, and David, to give them strength, sent them cheesecake." This of course was completely erroneous. It was cheese, not cheesecake. Saul was no kind of scholar.

They knew the original recipe was available in an English translation of Cato's boring book. They took it to Sally Baumberg, to whom Sarah had intended to go for their party cake the whole time. Sally made the best bar mitzvah cakes in New York and everyone knew it. She could create spun-sugar baseball players, ice skaters, even Torahs. Anything you wanted she could spin or pull. And the cake itself—this was not usual party cake. These cakes were too good to have only one piece of them. That's what Masha wanted. But when they showed Sally Cato's recipe, she read it quickly and shrieked. "Are you trying to ruin me? How can I serve this? This is chopped liver."

The Putzes didn't really understand. They had already ordered a sculpted chopped liver platter—two of them—from the caterer. They liked chopped liver.

. . .

Sally studied Cato's recipe. The more she thought about it, the more she became convinced that this was her chance to redefine New York cheesecake. Forget about Cato. She could be another Arnold Reuben—the Arnold Reuben of the twenty-first century. Reuben was a German Jew who had come to New York in the early twentieth century. He opened a restaurant that was famous for its sandwiches, although, strangely, he did not invent the Reuben sandwich. But he did invent a cheesecake made with cream cheese. At the time, cheesecake was supposed to be made with farmer's cheese, as it had been back in Germany. But cream cheese was more New York. His cheesecake became famous as *the* New York cheesecake. Nearly a century later, Sally had a vision of herself becoming famous for Cato's new New York cheesecake. But she could see that Cato's was not even edible. She would have to reinvent it the same way Reuben had.

Two weeks later, she sat the Putzes down and presented them with a platter of unfrosted cake slices. There was white, yellow, light chocolate, and dark chocolate.

"First," said Sally, "there is this tracta business. It won't work. What was this Cato? A senator? He didn't know from cake. It's like getting a recipe from Ed Koch. Let's start with a good cake. If Reuben could use cream cheese, I can use cake."

She passed around her samples. Pointing to the yellow one, she said, "I think this is a good choice. It's called a 'genoise' and it's light and buttery. The name means 'from Genoa.' That's not far from where Cato was. He probably knew this cake, though he clearly didn't know how to make it. He was a politician, not a baker."

No one was interested in challenging the logic of this. Sarah had to point out that a chocolate cake would work better with the ganache.

"We will get to the ganache in a minute," said Sally patiently. Her line of work required a great deal of patience. After they'd settled on the genoise, then came the cheese filling. Sally felt a certain historic pressure to use cream cheese. But no, she was blazing a new trail from ancient Rome to the Upper West Side. She proposed ricotta cheese. That would be more like Cato's sheep cheese. And she would mix it with mascarpone—Cato, she asserted, would have liked mascarpone—mixed with vanilla whipped cream. She would blend this with a custard of egg yolks and sugar and, to please Cato, a little sweet Marsala wine. "Now *there* is a Roman cheese filling for you." The Putzes all agreed without suspicion of the derivative aspect; they didn't know the recipe for tiramisù.

Then came the chocolate cake and the rich chocolate layer of ganache. Sally had no problem with ganache. If Reuben could make his mark with cream cheese, couldn't she make hers with ganache? After the genoise would come the cheese filling, then chocolate cake, then a layer of ganache. Then a thin dark chocolate cake layer. Sally was inventing. There were to be three tiers, each a third smaller in diameter than the last. "Now," said Sally, rubbing her hands. "How do we glaze it? Cato said honey. Maybe that's all he had. We can do better."

"Buttercream," said Masha. "Maybe vanilla buttercream?" She said it as if she were answering a quiz.

"Listen," said Sally, who in her mind was fighting for a career-defining move. "We've got an ancient Roman cake. Oldest recipe in the world. Some adults are going to find that interesting, but for kids, this cake is going to have to look irresistible. So how do you sell a cake? Anyone who has ever had a shop or restaurant knows this answer. Hmm?"

The Putzes had no answer.

"Sarah, I'm surprised at you. You can sell anything if you cover it in chocolate. We cover it with a shiny dark chocolate glaze. Dark chocolate, confectioners' sugar, a little cream for shine. Definitely no honey."

The Putzes looked delighted. They were getting excited.

"Then I can make a few pillars and Roman arches out of spun sugar. The white will look great against the dark glaze," said Sally, nearly shouting in triumph.

"And what about the green crystals," said Saul, excitedly. "Adara had green crystals."

"We use green M&Ms," said Masha.

Everyone froze and stared at Masha in silence.

"Sure," Sarah said apologetically, knowing she was a customer, after all. "A good sprinkling of them. M! Get it? M for Masha."

They all laughed. "That's brilliant," said Saul.

They had no idea how brilliant it was, Masha thought. There was no better way to bait Rachel Rabbinowitz than with M&Ms. M&Ms were to Rachel what breasts were to Fabricio Bonatelli. The clear path to ruin.

. . .

When her day of haftarah and ganache finally came, Masha began the ceremony by reading the preselected passage from Samuel, in which Samuel, or Saul, was instructed to slaughter people because they had been mean to the Hebrews as they were fleeing Egypt. Masha could not resist adding that Moses had been pretty mean to them also, but she didn't dwell on it. Saul slaughtered the Amalekites, "but he spared the best of the sheep and cattle, the fat calves and lambs—everything that was good." What could be learned from this? "Here on West Eighty-Sixth Street," said Masha, "there are some pretty mean people, but we have to remember that some of them have wonderful dogs. We have to show kindness and love to their dogs."

Quite a few people in the synagogue, including her grandmother Ruth, could not make much sense of this message, but fortunately no one else was listening. The others congratulated Ruth, noting that Masha stood upright at the bimah, her voice was loud and clear, and she kept her hair off her face. They had all been conditioned to listen to language that they did not understand—Hebrew, Aramaic. They could appreciate the delivery but did not concern themselves with the content, even in English. Rabbi Pinkerman knew this. He wondered if anyone listened to anything he was saying. He would occasionally insert a mild criticism of Israel. Then he would find out which ones were listening. Some were.

Diane Davis had the gracefulness to drift her way through a crowded bat mitzvah reception. She congratulated Masha and talked to a few of her students, including Rachel. Rachel wanted the other kids to see this famed woman with whom she was intimately chatting. But to most of the others she was just chatting with some well-dressed, really, really skinny woman. That was all right with Masha. She knew Rachel was living with the fact that Diane Davis had come to her event and not Rachel's. Some of the adults were ballet fans and were excited to meet her, even though they gossiped relentlessly about how skinny she was.

"Too thin."

"Looks like a skeleton."

"Doesn't she ever eat?"

"Is she eating now?"

"I'm going to help her," declared Linda.

Oh no, thought everyone else.

Linda walked right up, hooked herself around Diane's bony arm, and got to the point. "Your arm is so skinny," she said. "Thank you," replied Diane without the slightest hint of irony—or anything else. Diane looked desperately for a nearby rescuer but there was no one except Saul, who would start pushing his television special if she invited him into the conversation. *Why would a food show interest a ballerina?*

"You ought to eat more," said Linda, needing no response as she pushed on and led Diane to a table with mountains of chopped liver. *Who is this woman and what is she selling?* thought Diane. The chopped liver had been sculpted into the shape of birds but had now collapsed into headless hills. Linda took a knife, spread some on a cracker, and handed it to Diane, who took it with her long fingers. It was like feeding a spider.

"Do you eat chopped liver?"

Diane helplessly shook her head. She was about to bravely take a bite when Linda said, "It's the schmaltz that makes it so healthy."

"Schmaltz?"

"Schmaltz. You know, chicken fat."

Diane Davis, whose name had not been Diane Davis until she became a ballerina, was a phony. She knew what schmaltz was. It had always nauseated her, seeing those little jars of yellow glob in her mother's refrigerator. She only had nostalgia for one food. Her family used to go to Delancey Street, sometimes to Second Avenue or even Fourteenth Street, to eat New York cheesecake. It had a real cookie crust, not graham cracker, and glazed fresh strawberries on top. But everything was closed now. The Lower East Side was becoming a land of cupcake stores. Cupcakes were meaningless. Just pretty and pointless, like a bad date. Now cheesecake was coming back on West Eighty-Sixth Street, which, for Diane Davis, was the most exciting thing since the opera left midtown and moved up. But was it real cheesecake? She had heard words like "authentic" and "original." Was this equal to the strawberry, or even the caramel pecan, cheesecake she remembered from Miss Grimble's when she was a little girl?

Violette's birthday had been a disappointment to Diane. The cheesecake had been, anyway. What did those people know? They weren't even Jewish. But they knew how to throw a party. With the help of absinthe, potent for someone who almost never drank, she had found other indulgences to enjoy—ones that didn't put on any weight. But now she only remembered that the cheesecake hadn't been right. (Besides, a man named Harold who said he was from "the birthday party" kept calling her. She didn't know who he was.) But Masha's event had promised "authentic" cheesecake, and since it was a Jewish event, they probably knew what that should be. She would avoid all this chopped liver. Her one indulgence would be the cheesecake.

But there was Linda, practically forcing her to take liver and schmaltz. Fortunately, Linda finally spotted Saul and descended on him with a "great idea." This was the life of a television producer: Everyone wants to talk to you except the people you want to talk to. Saul wore a well-tailored dark blue Armani suit with an Armani purple tie. Armani was to Saul what truffle oil was to Art. Most people wouldn't know what it was, but the ones who recognized it were the ones you wanted to impress.

Diane was able to gracefully abandon her cracker at a deserted table. Saul pretended to engage with Ruth Arnstein and then left Linda with Ruth, abandoned as gracefully as the unwanted chopped liver. Linda talked to Ruth about the brilliance of Masha's talk, although when Ruth cruelly asked her what it had been about, Linda shifted to why "that ballerina" was so skinny. Ruth was thinking about how her physical therapist had promised that in a few weeks she could be rid of the walker and just use a cane. Then she'd be able to whack people over the head—this Linda, for example—with it.

. . .

Sally's moment, or was it Cato's, arrived. "Authentic Cato's cheesecake" was brought out. Everyone was once again informed that this was a delicacy from ancient Rome, the oldest known written recipe. And it was magnificent, as you might expect of a dish from Rome. The structure was three feet high, enrobed in glistening dark chocolate with white Roman columns and arches strategically placed over the three tiers, and green M&Ms randomly scattered on the landscape. When it was cut into, the cross section of light and dark cakes and light and dark fillings gave each piece zebra stripes. Surely Cato would have been impressed, but Diane concealed her disappointment. This may have been ancient Rome, but it wasn't Delancey Street or even Miss Grimble's. No one expected her to eat dessert anyway.

Slices were distributed on small plates, and Masha noted with satisfaction that Rachel circled back for a second slice.

She also managed to periodically cruise by to pick off an M&M or two. In all she got quite a few of them. Wait until the School of American Ballet sees her next week, thought the sly bat mitzvah girl.

. . .

Now everyone wanted Sally Baumberg's "Cato's New York cheesecake." It was prominently featured in her catalogue. It started to appear at the biggest bar mitzvahs and weddings on the Upper West Side. Sally could even offer M&Ms with different initials printed on them. Diners at Mykonos began to express disappointment that their Cato's cheesecake was nothing like Sally's.

Soon this new "Cato's cheesecake" was popular all over Manhattan, then Brooklyn. Bakeries started making imitations, always with the chocolate glaze, not honey, and rarely getting Sally's complex interior right. Then it popped up in San Francisco and from there in L.A. Could Seattle be far behind?

Sally hoped it would be called Baumberg's cheesecake, but it never was. Occasionally on the Upper West Side, especially by the younger crowd, it was called Masha's cheesecake. But usually it was known as Cato's cheesecake, with no distinction made between the wildly different versions. Sally, never one to fight a trend, had M&Ms made with either a C, an A, a T, or an O printed on them.

Sally posted the recipe online, although, like all great recipes, a few small secrets were left out. You had to go to Baumberg's if you wanted the real thing. She didn't leave out nearly as much as Cato had, though. Sally understood what the senator had been doing. Maybe Baumberg's Cato's New York cheesecake *could* become as famous as Reuben's.

One of the few sour notes in all of this was from Ruth Arnstein. She kept pointing out that in Cato's day, no one in Rome had ever seen or tasted chocolate. For all the greatness of Rome, there had been no ganache. And even without supporting documentation, it seemed unlikely that Cato had had M&Ms.

15

The Last Night

Today Hoffman would rhyme one of his special words, autokabalesis. It is the act of suicide by jumping, which is something you have to do right.

> A man turned to autokabalesis
> Because he received not nearly enough kisses . . .
> If it's too low a jump
> You receive but a bump
> And you get no points for near misses.

Was there no market for such brilliance? he thought. No. He had put in a lot of research. He was a good researcher. He was trying to find out the minimum number of floors that would ensure success. He found that many people survived jumping from great altitudes. Others died at slight heights. It depends.

It depends. It depends. That is the only serious answer for a serious question.

Hoffman would have preferred the roof, but the door leading to it was locked. On the worst day of your life there's no reason to expect anything to go right. He opened his living room window with a contrived resolve. The roof was only one story up, but still, that would've been higher, more certain. This was the shortest building on the block. The fifth-floor window would have to do. It should be good enough. He prayed that it would be.

He had to climb over the black window guard that the city required in all apartments with children. Hoffman had no children. It must have been installed for some previous tenant. Now it was just in the way. Was he really doing this? Once over the guard, he lost his balance and didn't need to decide. It was windier than he'd expected and his hands slipped.

Five stories were enough. There was not a lot of blood and the body was quickly covered with a blanket. Police cars, police, reporters, photographers, and curious neighbors congregated on the block below the open window. No one knew who the man was, but several of them walked over to the doorman to ask if the jumper's apartment was a rental or a co-op. The police found his name and gave it to the reporters. If he had been identified as A. G. Hoffman, maybe someone would have remembered. Maybe the reporter from the *Times*. But the only thing that was known for certain about Albert Hoffman was that his apartment was now available.

If Ruth Arnstein had known Hoffman, she would have renounced tuna sandwiches. But she knew nothing of him or his choice for lunch. When Mimi found out what had happened, she seemed not as disturbed by what Hoffman had done as by the fact that she didn't even know who he was. She had never even heard anything about him. Her first question was, "Did he have a dog"? She might know the dog.

"Who was Hoffman?" she would ask from time to time of people on the block.

"Hoffman?"

"You know, the guy who jumped." No one knew him.

Ruth said she thought that she had talked to him once. "Really?" said Mimi.

"You know, he was that far-darter who never said anything. I passed him for twenty years and he never said hello. So one morning I said 'good morning.' You know what he said?"

"What?" asked Mimi.

"He asked me if I knew a good rhyme for cheesecake."

"Cheesecake . . . tease fake."

"What is tease fake?"

"I don't know. It rhymes."

. . .

Mimi had much to sell. Both the Chillida and the Tàpies were already sold. The market was good for Spanish abstractionists. She thought of selling her famous piano. Musicians always wanted to play that piano, and wherever she was going, she was not going to have a big enough space for concerts. She was not going to have space for anything. She thought of selling the Chihuly. What would her home be without its tintinnabulation? But she wouldn't have a high enough ceiling. The trapeze would be gone, too. She thought of the Indian calf—were those real sapphires? It would be bad luck to sell it. By the time she found a two-thousand-dollar-a-month apartment in Hoboken, New Jersey, she had already passed the time when she was supposed to move and Art was threatening eviction. The new place had two bedrooms—maybe one could be a dining room—but there would not be room for events, and anyway the kitchen was small.

She still had just one more thing to do before she moved—the last famous dinner party. And it would feature a giant cheesecake, the best cheesecake West Eighty-Sixth Street had ever seen. It had been taking time to organize—more time than the merry Greeks, with their warm smiles of rejection, wanted to allow her. The Greeks were at the end of their patience. Art seemed anxious to get into the apartment. When she sent out invitations, Art declared she would have to move out the day after. This left her wondering when she would pack. She could figure that out after her last great event.

She would have Shannon Lynch, a musical prodigy from Galway, Ireland, on the piano. Shannon loved Chopin. His music could be sweet, but it lasted because it was also sorrowful. He had liked minor keys—the Nocturne in C Minor, the Prelude in E Minor, that Ballade in G Minor. And the saddest key of all for the Prelude in D Minor. Shannon claimed that the Irish understood the sadness underneath beauty and said that Chopin resembled Irish poetry. She would play Chopin while thinking of the Irish tragedy, playing on Rubenstein's piano, and Mimi would invite people to hear her. Mimi had launched careers before, and this was one last try.

She would also invite some young authors and old agents and Ti Auguste, of course. She would invite critics and gallery owners and art figures that could be important for him to meet. This was her last chance. Maybe Chihuly would come? But he was in Seattle, and anyway it would be awkward with her planning to sell his piece. Maybe he would want to buy it back?

Ti Auguste did not want to meet the important people Mimi was lining up for him. He had been avoiding them for years. They would increase his prices, increase his sales, and soon he would lose his rent stabilization just like Mimi had. That was Mimi's whole problem, according to Ti Auguste. She didn't understand that in New York, success is always to be avoided.

Mimi would invite Michael Klein, who had been at a number of her parties. Tough-talking Michael, a veteran city politician and a formidable presence, was the Manhattan borough president. He always said he would "do something" about rent stabilization. What something was he doing? Maybe he had promised the Greeks he would do something too, but that would have been a different "something." Mimi wanted to ask him at her last party.

She had to invite Gerta—Gerta Hollman and her husband, Joshua Pinsky. She had introduced them. He was a cellist with the New York Philharmonic and she was a violinist whose only work, other than giving lessons, was making strudel. She had worked at Lichtman's on Eighty-Sixth on the other side of Amsterdam, but when the landlord quadrupled the rent, the shop was gone. To find new work, she had to travel up

Amsterdam to Morningside Heights to the last Hungarian bakery. She was a good strudel maker and they hired her. It was also the secret to her marriage. Josh knew many young attractive violinists, but what Mimi knew about Josh was that above all else, more than he loved Bach, Dvořák, and Bruch, he loved strudel. So this was a perfect shidduch.

. . .

Ruth and Mimi had in common a distaste for what they called "fake food." As Ruth put it, "You can't get a bunch of seafood and throw it in a soup and call it bouillabaisse." Over the years Mimi had debunked a number of popular recipes. When she'd owned her catering service she'd made real red velvet cake from a hundred-year-old recipe that had nothing in common with the fake red velvet made today, full of red food coloring. She'd used unprocessed cocoa powder, which naturally turns red, only it didn't seem to turn as red as food coloring. Her customers thought her red velvet wasn't red enough.

For one dinner party she had made real coq au vin. There is no reason to stew a young hen for hours in wine. The recipe is for a coq, a rooster, which is hard to find in New York markets. Rooster meat is tough and gamey, but after hours of stewing it yields a soft, flavorful meat. Most of her guests hadn't really liked it and had been disappointed that it wasn't the usual coq-less coq au vin.

They didn't like her gefilte fish that Passover either. Gefilte fish means "stuffed fish," and Mimi made it the original way: a big poached pike stuffed with ground whitefish, minced carp, chopped onions, and herbs. This was real Jewish cooking, because what could cause more suffering than deboning a pike, the world's boniest fish? She presented it on a platter in cut slices. Nobody even understood that it was gefilte fish because they expected to have poached fish balls, a handmade imitation of an industrial fake.

Now Ruth and Mimi knew she had to make the real Cato's cheesecake.

"I was there at its launch."

"Where was that?"

"Masha Putz's bat mitzvah."

"A Saul Putz production?"

"Exactly. It was for kids. But there were a lot of adults. Diane Davis was there."

"Diane Davis. I once invited her to a dinner party and she wouldn't eat anything." Mimi snorted her disapproval. "So I don't invite her anymore. It's like a pub crawl with a teetotaler."

"Yeah, it was a kids' party anyway, so they made the Cato cake with lots of chocolate, M&Ms. Nothing to do with Cato's recipe."

"You have the recipe? The original?"

"I'll show you. I don't eat it, of course."

This was Mimi's kind of challenge.

. . .

Mimi always invited the residents of her building, "the real New Yorkers, the landsleit." But she only included the old tenants. She didn't know the new ones and they didn't know her. Besides, they didn't look like real New Yorkers and they didn't talk to her because they had their headphones on, but once word of her party spread, the new ones actually holstered their Walkmans and started talking to her in hopes of an invitation. "Who was Hoffman?" was always a good icebreaker. Everyone was certain she would be the one to know. But she didn't.

"See this," Ruth said to Mimi, holding up a black cane. "No more walker."

"That's right. So I can come to the party without blocking half the room. But just keep that pisher Linda away." She held up the cane. "I swear to god, I'll whack her one."

"Linda? Linda who?"

"You know Linda. Linda, ahh—I don't know. Linda. Linda the pisher."

"Oh," said Mimi. "Linda."

"What is she, a French movie star? Why doesn't she have a last name?" Mimi shrugged. "Are you inviting her? If she talks to me she's going to get whacked."

"I'll tell her not to talk to you." And Mimi really was going to tell her. She couldn't have people whacked with canes at her party.

But Linda was always invited. She was a divorcée, crowded into a two-bedroom on the fourth floor with her large son and daughter and three generally disagreeable fox terriers. The son and daughter should have moved off by now but they were still there. The foxes liked Linda and no one else. Mimi knew all three terriers by name—each snarled differently— but even the old tenants had no idea about the names of the now large children.

Linda's face was always frozen in a scowl, not unlike her dogs'. Mimi thought it could've been the look on her face when her husband asked for a divorce, so long ago that Mimi couldn't remember him, and had just never gone away. Mimi always tried to say things that would make Linda's face change, but they never worked.

Some months earlier, during a hot spell, Linda's air conditioner had broken down. She'd started spending her days in the lobby treating the day doorman, Federico, to endless questions. How many BTUs was the lobby air conditioner? Would it fog up the marble walls? Does air-conditioning stave off bedbugs? Can they come in the doorway? What is there to stop the mice? Finally Federico had arranged for someone to fix her air-conditioning.

She's not dumb, thought Mimi. *There is a cleverness to irritating people. That is why they are so irritating.*

"So who's coming to your party?" Linda asked the next time she saw Mimi, assuming she was invited.

"Ruth Arnstein is coming and she's carrying a cane and she's mad at you, so stay away from her."

"Why is she mad at me? I just saw her at the bat mitzvah."

"I'm telling you, she's dangerous with her new cane and you have to stay away from her. A cane's distance away."

Linda took a rare two seconds of silence to absorb this message and then bravely smiled. "So who else is coming?"

"Well," said Mimi, attempting a kind of coyness that was not really in her repertoire. "Mick Jagger is coming."

Mimi knew the second the words were out that she would regret saying them. Linda only scowled back. It was a failure. It hadn't changed her face. But Linda told every person she encountered—hairdressers, dog walkers, bank tellers, frozen yogurt dispensers. Soon everyone on the Upper West Side, possibly all of Manhattan, knew that Mick Jagger was coming to Mimi's party, making it *the* party to which you had to be invited.

It was not beyond possibility. Mimi really did know Mick Jagger. She knew everyone—except Hoffman. Jagger had lived in the neighborhood and had thrown parties that were said to be even better than hers. People described his parties as "wild," but nobody really knew what that meant, just like the phrase "a wild woman" alerts everyone's attention but eludes everyone's understanding. Mimi had come to know him as a kind and caring man and didn't understand when people called him wild. He'd often been heard graciously saying that Mimi Landau threw the best parties in the neighborhood, but he'd never gone to one.

He no longer lived in the neighborhood but she invited him anyway, through his press agent. He responded, "If I am in New York, I will definitely come." Poor Mick, Mimi thought. He never knows where he is. This made him the exact opposite of her.

"Who was Hoffman?" became the code of the new stiffly dressed people in the building—men with expensive leather bags, women with headphones dancing to music no one else could hear. People who never held a door or said hello on an elevator suddenly wondered what Mimi knew about Hoffman. They must have expected to begin an extravagant conversation that would lead to an invitation to her Mick Jagger party. But she was tiring of explaining that she knew nothing about Hoffman and this opening led nowhere.

. . .

Gerta, who had come to Mimi's to start preparing for the party, thought Mimi should have invited some of the new people in the building. "You have to live with them," she said.

"No, I won't," she said, with a smile so suddenly bitter it was like pain had flared up in her molar. She had invited her dentist, hoping it might lead to a price break on an implant she desperately needed, but this spread would probably convince him that she could pay full price. Still, it was her conviction that every party should have a dentist, but no party should have two.

"Oh, I found some good soft sheep cheese," Gerta said, "for Cato." Mimi smiled, remembering how much her poodle had loved cheese.

"What are you going to do with all this stuff?"

Mimi shrugged.

"When do you have to be out?"

"Last week I think. Want a pinball machine?"

While they were working in the kitchen, Josh was doing pull-ups on the trapeze and wishing he could do something more impressive. Mimi stroked the calf as she passed by but the magic didn't seem to work anymore.

They had placed Cato's book, open to the cheesecake recipe, on the kitchen island. Mimi could not get the dough in the recipe to work. It was heavy, hard, and crumbly. "The senator didn't know how to make a good dough," said Gerta. "How many senators even today make good dough?" They laughed.

Gerta, meanwhile, made strudel dough, light, soft, and elastic. With the glass sculpture jingling by the door, she stretched it as thin as tissue on the tops of her forearms while her fists pounded the flour-dusted canvas on the table to produce the stretching motion. Then she brushed it with melted butter, one sheet on top of another, until she had a thick pastry of many layers, light as dried meringue. The recipe had called for oil but Gerta's only argument was "butter is better."

"Butter is always better," said Mimi. "That's what's wrong with the Mediterranean." She forced the sheep cheese through a sieve and then mixed it with honey.

Now they had a dough that worked. They tossed out Mimi's disastrous attempt, or was it Cato's. They put down five buttered pastry sheets and a third of the cheese mixture, then five more sheets and another third. Another five layers were placed on top, and then the rest of the cheese and a few more sheets of pastry. Then Gerta wrapped the entire thing in four remaining buttered sheets so it was completely covered. She buttered the top and brushed it with beaten egg yolk so that it would brown and carefully placed it in an oven of only 350 degrees. No higher—Mimi warned her the big oven ran a little hot.

Once their confection had cooled, they added a light honey glaze, as Cato had ordered, that gave a polished shine to the golden surface. It was not exactly Cato's recipe, Mimi admitted. But Cato's version was full of flaws. "You have to interpret and make it work. But I don't substitute with pointless frauds," she asserted. "Just some improvements. No hens for roosters!"

Gerta agreed because she could see that Mimi wanted her to. Mimi's apartment would be gone and so would she, but she would be remembered for her cheesecake. Cato had proven that cheesecake is never forgotten. Hers would be the best on West Eighty-Sixth Street.

Mimi made little caviar canapés and endive stuffed with Roquefort and pears—her favorite foods. She made her coulibiac of salmon, layering the last fresh wild coho salmon available this year atop sliced mushrooms and hard-boiled eggs all tied together with ropelike vesiga and then wrapped in a French brioche dough and baked. It was the last of her vesiga, made in Russia from the spines of sturgeons, dried and needing to be soaked back to life. Dried it would keep forever, but for what was she saving it? It had been used for coulibiacs all the time in the old days, but this might be her last ever. She had always bought the vesiga from Sammy Grodno in his chaotic shop on 131st and Broadway. He too was a last—said to be the last Jew in an old Jewish section of Harlem. He'd died a few years earlier and his shop full of fish and pickles had closed. She liked to collect the last of things. People had stopped eating vesiga years earlier because it was considered bad luck: It was said to have been served in a soup on the *Titanic.*

An Upper West Side Apicius, she was making luxury food, so truffles could not be far behind. In the tradition of Apicius, she spent more than she could afford for two black truffles. The flavor was subtle but some might appreciate it. For Mimi the point was that it was one of the few foods that was truly black, and Mimi loved black. Brillat-Savarin, the Frenchman born in the mid-eighteenth century who was one of the first food writers and launched the truffle fashion, once wrote of Adam and Eve, "Parents of the human race, you have lost everything for an apple. What would you not have done for a truffled turkey?" Truffled turkey. The question had intrigued Mimi and so she'd presented the dish at her next Thanksgiving. But she'd had to announce it for her guests to be impressed, and the mystique had been not the flavor but how much she had spent. To use truffles was extravagant. If truffles had been affordable, people would rather have eaten lox. For this final party, she knew her crowd: A few would be impressed with the pâté annotated with black musty spots. But it was the cheesecake, as Apicius might have said, that would be declared "to die for"—she hoped.

She made her special lamb paprikás with real Hungarian paprika, the last from the green-and-red square tin, and great gobs of sour cream and a sprinkling of tangy caraway. Guests could scoop a few spoonfuls on a plate from the big flowered ovenproof tureen and take a dumpling from the long tray where they marched three abreast like a scout parade. From two jars of apricots that she had put up in brandy—no point in keeping them any longer—she made small tartlettes. There were also little hors d'oeuvres of young sheep cheese beaten with butter and dusted with chopped dill and fine rare Mediterranean anchovies from Collioure, where they used to be plentiful—another last. Then she made a Dobos torte with ten paper-thin layers of sponge cake between light chocolate buttercream. On top were the triangular caramel wedges all arranged on the same slant so that they looked like the fans of a Candyland turbine.

Of course, Dorothy, 5B, would probably spend all night drifting through the room, shouting, "So where's the lox?" She always did this, but Mimi always invited her anyway. Why didn't she bring her own lox? Mimi should've put BYOL on the invitation and seen what happened. Dorothy still wasn't as annoying as the couple in 12C who took a week in Paris every year and went from table to table saying, "Delicious! Let's get some at Fauchon next year."

For wine, she served the world's best Riesling: Trockenbeerenauslese from the Rheingau. Its fruity dryness and rich flavor were unlike any other. She and Arnold had bought two cases that she kept chilled as though he would come back at any moment to share some. But she knew he wouldn't, so it was time to drink it. She remembered his scientific explanation of how the berries were aged and shriveled to produce this rare intensity. The only problem with serving Rheingau wine was that 2A had recently cruised the Rhine. Mimi knew this would be their excuse to tell her about it.

There were also two bottles of fourteen-year-old grappa from Schiavon in Vicenza province. She and Arnold had actually bought these bottles twenty-two years earlier, so she was not sure if the grappa could properly be called fourteen years old or thirty-six.

Guests would bring desserts, but they wouldn't be interesting. She'd always been given almond kugelhopf from the German bakery on the East Side and poppyseed cakes from Second Avenue, but all those places were gone now. Maybe Hoffman had been the last German. Who was the last Jew left? Or the last Italian in Little Italy? No one ate spumoni anymore, and now that you could get espresso anywhere, was there any point to Little Italy? Black people were disappearing from Harlem and Ti Auguste was surely the last Haitian in her neighborhood. Where had all those people gone? Mimi fantasized about living in a house that held the last people driven out of all the neighborhoods living together. Maybe they could share vesiga soup before the ship finally sank.

. . .

It was getting dark. Gerta and Josh could look after things before the guests started coming, Mimi thought. She wanted to take a walk down the block. Was this her last evening in the neighborhood?

But as soon as she got onto the street she could see plainly that it was not *her* neighborhood anymore. Most of the landsleit were gone. The dogs, and the people walking them, were strangers. The only people she knew were the doormen, some of whom she had known for more than twenty years. A hello at each awning. The smokers were all lined up, young men addicted to tobacco who foolishly bought into co-ops that did not allow smoking. They were all men. Their wives didn't seem to smoke. One tall blond man wore a blue Yale T-shirt but didn't look old enough to have graduated. He was smoking a long thick cigar, which, according to the band, was a Montecristo. Maybe not a real one from Cuba, but the name carried weight. Everyone has their own truffle oil.

There were more newcomers on the block. Small herds of rats noiselessly galloped across the sidewalk to the gutter like fast-moving shadows. Yale threw his still-lit cigar stub, creating a flash as the lit end hit the sidewalk and silhouetting a rapidly vanishing thin black tail. Why were rats on West Eighty-Sixth Street? They used to stay on the smaller streets with less traffic. Lazarus, a keen observer of rat life, knew the answer. It was because there were more and more rich people here. The more rich people, the more food thrown out. Good for him and good for rats.

A wild-eyed man with a familiar face walked up to Mimi and said, "Fuck you!"

"You too," Mimi responded with a warm smile. Then she returned to her apartment, where guests would soon be arriving. Linda might already be there.

16

No Satisfaction

When Mimi got back, Gerta and Joshua were placing candles around the large room. When the Greeks took over the building, they redid all utilities and paid for them as a part of their operating expenses. Tenants were pleased to no longer pay gas and electricity bills but soon realized that this allowed the landlords to raise their rent. The move pushed many apartments closer to the level at which the Greeks could examine income and cut off rent stabilization.

Mimi had never used much electricity because she preferred candlelight and disliked air-conditioning. Cato had sometimes knocked over candles, so she had needed to be alert; but now the danger was gone, proving her theory that a rich life is one in which there are risks. She claimed that using candles reduced her carbon footprint and helped reduce climate change, but she was not really sure this was true. Candles burn carbon, and electricity might be more efficient.

She had asked a chemist friend, Brian Everling, to run tests on carbon emission from candles. Everling loved setting up such tests, but he said that so far, his work was inconclusive.

They set the main room with fifty-seven large candles, substantial wax columns that could last the night. The room would have a quivering golden glow, browned out at the edges, and ordinary people would acquire a classical gravity, a depth and importance, a slight whiff of beauty.

Even Linda had a kind of ethereal glow in candlelight when she arrived first, looking for Mick Jagger. She didn't want him to arrive and leave before she came. She did not know that arriving first was one on a list of differences between her and Mick. She noted with relief that Ruth, with her new cane, had not yet arrived either. What if Mick came with Ruth and she could not approach him without getting within smacking distance of Ruth?

Alice Lisker, the official poet laureate of New York State, arrived with her husband, a warm man whom Mimi enjoyed talking to because he was an astronomer. Mimi thought that poet and astronomer was the perfect recipe for marriage. Alice resembled a wren, beautiful but with alert eyes that darted around the room. Mimi had met her while walking Cato on Riverside Drive. Riverside Drive with its birds and flowers had been a special treat for Cato, for both of them.

How wonderful, thought Mimi, that New York State gets its own poet. She thought New York City should have its own, too. How could Manhattan and Rensselaer have the same one? Alice was really the Poet Laureate of the Upper West Side since much of her poetry was set there. Eighty-Sixth Street should have its own poet laureate, thought Mimi. There should be one for the block between

Amsterdam and Columbus. She thought landlords should be required to have at least one poet in every building so that every block could compete for its own poet laureate. It was fun to imagine imposing maddening rules on landlords.

Mimi was not surprised that Alice wanted to know about Hoffman. It might have become a poem, except that Mimi did not have a story to offer her. Alice gave her a copy of her newest book, *Cross Walks*. Mimi carefully placed the book on a counter in the kitchen next to a paper bag from the hardware store. Mimi refused to use plastic bags anymore.

Brian Everling arrived, looked around the curling candlelight. "A lot of carbon."

"But more than electricity?" Mimi probed

Everling gave the standard scientific answer, "Yes and no." Mimi nodded to say she wanted to hear it. Scientists learn to wait for the nod. "The first question is what kind of electric plant you're drawing from. If it's solar you'd better blow out the candles now. But oil? Coal? Then there is the issue of the kind of candles. They are not all the same either. Some have more efficient wicks, made of different materials." He paused to see if Mimi was ready to retreat. She wasn't. "Ironically, light is measured in units called candles. A lightbulb almost always puts out more candles than a candle. A lightbulb that puts out fifteen candles is more efficient than fifteen candles. The bulb will usually burn less carbon per candle, unless maybe it's drawing from a coal-fired plant. So the question is, how much light do you need? We should try to get by with less light. If you only need one candle of light, just use one candle. But this is a lot of candles."

"Fifty-seven."

"Really?"

This was why Mimi loved to talk science. You always learned a great deal but ended up knowing nothing. Science is the art of uncertainty.

"I'll miss these parties," said Borough President Michael Klein. Mimi would have been too polite to point out that it would not have been the last if he had done something about rent destabilization. She didn't have to because several people from the building were grabbing him to complain about it already. Klein, like his pressed suit, was not easily disrupted. With avuncular calm he pointed out that the city codes were "a complete mishmash." That was it for Ruth. Klein was trying to sound ethnic but she hated people who said "mishmash" when the word was "mishmosh." Ruth's conversational Yiddish was probably not much good anymore since there was no one left with whom to converse. But they could at least get the words right.

Joshua played Ernest Bloch's *Schelomo* on his plaintive cello, which was not bright party music, though perhaps it was a good background song for a discussion of rents. There was enough of a crowd to introduce Shannon Lynch and announce that she was going to be playing Chopin on the very piano Rubenstein had used.

After Shannon played, Saul Putz reached up and brushed his fingertips against Chihuly's glass as though it were a harp. It was his way of taking ownership because he had agreed to buy the piece from Mimi. He sat down on the piano bench and played some bars of Schumann. He played like an acceptable music student who would never have a career. Ruth, who sat next to him on the bench because she needed a place to sit, was amazed at the way such rich people could get away with anything. Anyone who played like Saul would never dare play in public unless they were rich. Saul Putz was not embarrassed by his few measures of Schumann, which in fact was sadder than Chopin (but not when played by Saul).

"You know," he said to Ruth. "I think I might buy this piano too."

Sure, thought Ruth, *and then you can play it however you want.* But she didn't say that. She said, "Why don't you change the spelling of your name? Then people would pronounce it the way you want."

Saul smiled. "It wasn't our original name. They changed it at Ellis Island."

"What was it originally?" Ruth asked like a dutiful straight man.

"Schmuck."

Saul loved this joke and told it whenever he could. People had to laugh. It was the only polite response. Ruth had heard it before. Sometimes he used schlemiel. But Ruth knew that her son-in-law was no schlemiel. New Yorkers were not schlemiels—no matter what landlords and politicians might think. New Yorkers pride themselves on not being schlemiels. Ruth was not alone in thinking "schlemiel" and "out-of-towner" were interchangeable terms as witnessed by the influx of new schlemiels in the building. *Let's get it right,* Ruth thought. The truth was, Saul was a putz but he was not a schmuck. She had a fine eye for such distinctions. These words matter. Saul is a putz and Klein is a schmuck. You can love a putz but you can't love a schmuck.

While Ruth was weighing the proper term for Saul, Linda was watching from a distance. She wanted to talk to Saul. She had an idea for him. But she was afraid of Ruth.

Mimi swallowed her natural fear of people with reverse names and went up to Webster Thomas to show him Ti Auguste's paintings on her wall. After he seemed either duly impressed or polite, she took him across the room to the corner where Ti Auguste was hiding. He had just been thinking that white people and their money were going to get him thrown out of his home, so he hid by talking to Linda, whom everyone avoided. Mimi was looking for people to introduce to Shannon or Ti Auguste. A last chance to make connections. Joshua joined Ethan Wright at the grand piano. Ethan was a bigger draw than Chopin this year with two hits on Broadway, neither of which Mimi had bothered to see. Now he was improvising hot, not cool, jazz on the piano, with Josh on cello and Gerta on violin.

While they were improvising, Webster managed to propose to Ti Auguste a show at his downtown gallery. Ti Auguste said he would think about it, then ran to Mimi to ask what she thought of agreeing to the show but only taking a small percentage of sales prices. Mimi laughed. "You're probably every art dealer's dream. Besides, you can't keep depending on me."

"Why not?" answered the painter. "Just because you're changing apartments?"

. . .

The soft tintinnabulation of hanging glass, like sleigh bells at the opening of a Russian movie, announced the coming of the Cato cheesecake, Gerta carrying it on a large New England maple cutting board. The cake came out turban-shaped with a polished copper finish looking like it belonged to the same cult as Mimi's bronze calf. Mimi set the shiny cake on the long table to warm applause. Despite their clapping, most recognized that this was not at all what Cato's cheesecake was supposed to be like. No chocolate. No flecks of green.

Each guest had a long thin champagne flute in which chilled Pol Roger was furiously bubbling upward as though futilely attempting escape. There were sixty-three guests but she had eighty champagne flutes. *How stupid*, she thought, *that a woman with eighty champagne flutes would be asked to move to a small kitchen in New Jersey.*

This was the moment, but she did not want to dwell on it for too long. No testimonials and certainly no talk of how this was the last Mimi soirée. No reflections on evenings past. Unbearable. This was New York. Couldn't it just be about cheesecake?

Gerta carefully sliced the cake, revealing feathery layers of pastry and earthy-tasting honey-sweet cheese. If she ever made this cake again she would perfume the cheese layer with orange blossom water.

Mimi raised her flute, looked at the cheesecake, and simply said, "To Cato." Wide-eyed and open-mouthed, everyone lifted their flutes and repeated, "To Cato." Mimi sipped her cold champagne with its kind and gentle bubbles and remembered Cato's soft black wool between her fingers. Cato's cheesecake was a success. It was something special, and her guests were eating it in utter silence. The only voice she heard was Dorothy's somewhere behind her saying, "So this is it? There's no lox?"

This might have been the first time a right-wing politician was ever toasted at Mimi's party. She preferred to think she was toasting the memory of her Cato. Only when researching the cheesecake had she discovered that Cato had been a right-wing warmonger who abused his wife and his servants. The lesson, she thought, is to never name those you love after politicians. You will always find out why later.

Mimi had hoped for some interesting musings from her guests on the subject of cheesecake. They were, after all, New Yorkers—old New Yorkers. The new ones probably never thought about cheesecake. But the only thoughts on the subject came from Linda, who pointed out how different this was from "the original" Cato's cheesecake she'd eaten at Masha's bat mitzvah. Ruth's cane was itching.

It was well past midnight and no one was leaving. A few were still arriving. Every time someone did, eyes darted toward the door in hopes of seeing Mick Jagger. At one point there was a fuss at the doorway and Linda nearly knocked guests over to be the first to greet Mick. But instead it was Naomi, the art critic, with a new and stunning lover whom she wore like a new dress. She was confused by the way there seemed to be tremendous excitement about their arrival and then indifference, even disappointment. Was her lover not up to expectations?

. . .

Eventually guests began leaving. Even Linda, realizing Mick was a no-show, left. Mimi moved through the room snuffing out candles with her thumb and forefinger. She looked at her blackened fingertip and muttered, "Carbon."

Looking back at the disheveled room in the first light of dawn from the kitchen doorway, she was reminded of Pompeii. There had been life, civilization, human activity, and suddenly it all had stopped—petrified by an unstoppable flow of lava, or, in this case, molten New York real estate interests. Champagne flutes on the tables rose like stalagmites. Some still held champagne, the bubbles all escaped. Some plates still held scraps of cheesecake. Other plates had remnants of hors d'oeuvres, even untouched canapés. It looked as though the guests had vanished mid-meal. Real life, petrified. There were two untouched slices of cheesecake left on the board.

It was difficult for Mimi to get used to the idea that food scraps could just be left out without Cato running wild through the room, gobbling things both edible and not, flutes and glasses crashing—the old scene that she had dreaded but would have loved right now instead of this funereal quiet. Cato would have loved his namesake cake. He'd loved bakery, loved cheese, and loved honey. These had been among his favorite items to steal. She stared at her living room, like a tourist among Pompeii's ruins. She was supposed to have moved days earlier—she could no longer remember how many. She looked at the piano, the paintings, the sculptures, the pinball machine, the trapeze, and the Chihuly hanging from the high ceiling.

Mimi went into the kitchen, closed the doors. Putting aside Alice's thin paperback of poetry, she removed a roll of thick, strong tape from the paper bag from the hardware store. It was gaffer's tape. She had once been a gaffer. (Well, she had worked for an off-off-Broadway company and had secured all the electrical cables to the floor with gaffer's tape just like this so that no one would trip over the cable.)

Funny, the things to which the mind runs. As she used the tape to seal the door and the windows, she thought again about Hoffman. *Who was Hoffman?* She took a Provençal café chair and placed it in front of the oven doors. The chair was one of a set of four in the corner of the kitchen, a bright Provençal blue with wicker seats that went with the small round table with flowers painted on it.

She picked up Alice's book and sat in front of the big cooking range, turning all the valves wide open. Mimi wished that she had written poetry. Poetry was a good thing to leave behind. What would she leave? Maybe she would be remembered for her cheesecake. This, after all, was New York . . . or it used to be. She began reading. Alice did not use urban metaphors. The crosswalks were crosswalks, white lines were white lines, a broken curb was a broken curb. It was just the city. A poem about a traffic light that felt like it was taking forever while she was stuck by the crosswalk.

And it did feel like forever. This was taking longer than she'd thought. She wasn't feeling light-headed or dizzy or faint in any way. She also didn't smell anything. Shouldn't there be a smell of gas? She didn't hear a hissing noise. Was she losing her sensations—first smell, then hearing?

In a sudden jolt of anger, she leapt to the light switches. She flipped them several times.

No light. No gas.

The landlords had cut off her utilities.

17

The Coup de Grâce

A rt could see that Niki and Adara had not completely assimilated to the new decade. This could be embarassing—a blow to the family standing. He bought them each Walkman players so they could listen to music, but they only wanted old Greek cassettes. Art hoped people could not hear how literally byzantine they were. Art refused to play their music in the restaurant. Worse, Adara made a recording of Cassandra's kids merrily bleating as she fed them milk. She said they were "happy sounds" that would put people in a good mood. Art refused to play that, either.

Despite the prediction that the world would be getting warmer, it was a cold winter. There was even a menacing dusting of snow. It was a stinging cold trash day. Lazarus, Old Mr. Boston, and a few others were sifting through the leavings, looking for wood or cardboard to burn in an empty garbage can for a little warmth. Lazarus found a painting in a thick wooden frame with good wooden stretchers. He ripped off the canvas and broke up the wood for use.

By now, Violette had rented the pied-à-terre from Art but didn't seem to use it much. But this mean winter morning, he knew she was in town, so Art called her and told her he needed to stop by in the afternoon for "a plumbing issue." She seemed to understand and told him that she would be there. When he rang the doorbell—he had had new ones installed in the building as part of the upgrade—Violette answered wearing a thin, almost fluid silk gown. Art was pretty sure she was wearing nothing underneath. This was going even better than he'd hoped.

The apartment seemed nearly empty. His fresh eggshell-white paint job was the only wall decoration. There was little furniture: a few chairs and a king-size bed with sheets and covers greatly disheveled. In the middle of the room was a wooden box about two feet high. And sitting in a corner was that sculptor, Sabino, whom he had met at Violette's birthday party. Art, who prided himself on powers of observation, could see what was happening. He fiddled with something on the radiator and said it was fine now and left. Alone again with Sabino, Violette dropped her robe and stood naked on the box as he translated her curvaceous body into a series of large, smooth gray clay cubes.

Back at Mykonos, Art once again hung the portrait of Cassandra in its pride of place next to the cheesecake photo. What were customers to make of the goat and the cheesecake, paired? Art didn't care. Adara was happy.

. . .

In the process of moving, Mimi had earned a substantial amount from selling her artwork. She had ended up keeping a few things—the piano, the pinball machine, the four remaining dessert woodcuts, the provincial table and chairs, and the eighty crystal champagne flutes. She had a goal in mind.

She was now living in Hoboken. It was not the amount of space she was used to, but it was bigger than anything she could afford in Manhattan. It had a sprawling living room and the two spacious bedrooms. Ironically—it was meant as a great perk but came off as a cruel irony—she had a view of Manhattan. She said this apartment was "fine," an easy commute to the city. In truth, it was difficult for her to even say the words "New Jersey." She didn't know the neighborhood or anyone in it and had no connection to this place. And if she wanted to throw parties, who would come out here? She only complained to Ruth. Ruth, of course, would never venture across the Hudson to lower buildings to visit her.

"Ruthie, there is no landsleit there. You know what I mean. Not a real neighborhood."

"Sure, kiddo. But the same thing is happening to Eighty-Sixth Street."

. . .

It was Gerta who saved Mimi with a plan. She explained to Mimi that there was a wealth of empty commercial spaces on the Upper West Side. The city gave such good breaks to landlords on unrented property that it was worthwhile to leave them empty. Landlords had begun demanding unreasonable rents and then, if there were no takers, making a profit on leaving the space vacant. The avenues were starting to resemble ghost towns. One of these now empty storefronts had until recently held the local chicken shop. Everyone had loved the chicken shop. The landsleit had, anyway. It had only sold delicious roasted chickens, but West Eighty-Sixth Street didn't have a chicken clientele anymore and the place had gone out of business. Gerta proposed to Mimi that they could rent the old chicken shop and make it into a bakery café specializing in their Cato's cheesecake, which was certain to have a following. They would even call the restaurant Cato's, both establishing their cheesecake as the authentic one and honoring her late poodle.

With some help from Gerta, who was to be her business partner, and with an affordable rent to maintain in New Jersey, she could afford the expense of the new venture. The rule for opening a restaurant is that you must have enough money to operate for a year without profit. Then you have a chance of survival. Mykonos could've operated for several years. Jay Mac didn't have enough money to survive three months and her future was uncertain despite the popularity of cheesecake macarons. But Mimi could make it. She felt that she was resurrecting her old neighborhood by establishing a great Eighty-Sixth Street cheesecake that wasn't made by landlords. The shop was just across Amsterdam from the old Hungarian bakery that the landlords had driven out. It didn't matter that she lived in New Jersey. The Greeks lived in Queens and Jay Mac lived in Brooklyn. The only commercial operator who actually lived on the block was Serafina.

It made the Greeks angry that she called her place Cato's, which made people think hers was the real cheesecake. Art wished he had thought of the name for their restaurant, but he was just grateful that his wasn't named after one of Adara's goats. Many people liked the idea that the Greeks had competition at the other end of the block. Horace assured her that if she drove in from New Jersey he could find her parking spots. He was astounded to learn that she didn't drive. Many old-time New Yorkers didn't. Ruth didn't drive either. She wished her husband hadn't. The old-time Manhattanites didn't have cars. They didn't have country homes to drive to.

In another sharp jab at the Greeks, Mimi had saved her remaining four dessert woodcuts and prominently displayed them in the café. But this backfired: She made the woodcuts famous in the neighborhood, so people became impressed that the Greeks had one too. Mimi and Gerta also found inexpensive copies of her Provençal table and chairs. The place had charm, gemütlichkeit.

At Cato's, Mimi was the host and Gerta the chef. Now Gerta was back, baking on the Upper West Side, across the street from where she'd started. Mimi convinced her to add to the repertoire poppyseed strudel, which Mimi had grown fond of. The more astute noticed that the poppyseed strudel took on Mimi's look. It had a black body and whitish pastry on top—Gerta did not bronze the pastry as she had her version of Cato's cheesecake. Mimi often joked to Ruth that Ruth should eat as much of it as she could now, because if Mimi died before her, poppyseed strudel would have to go on Ruth's no-order list.

But cheesecake was the star. People from not only the neighborhood but all over the West Side, and eventually even the East Side, liked to spend hours there sipping coffee, eating cheesecake, discussing. Mimi had also brought her piano, which Saul hadn't ended up buying after all, into the café, and good pianists, friends of Mimi, would come in and play. Sometimes Saul Putz would come by and play a little of his lifeless Schumann. But there was nothing anyone could do to stop him, and besides, maybe he would put them on TV. Joshua would bring his cello over on occasion and play Bach's second suite, Mimi's favorite because it was in D minor, which is the most sorrowful key and therefore the most Jewish.

Ruth, to show up the Greeks, fed pigeons in front of the café. They became part of the experience, perching uninvited on tables and chairs and even an occasional shoulder. But the breadcrumbs attracted rats, so she had to stop.

That model came in. Mimi recognized her from the neighborhood. Mimi had heard that she had left. But she seemed to be back. She was the subject of a famous painting, of which Mimi was not a fan. She was almost certain that the thick-built man with forearms like logs was the Basque sculptor Sabino Begotxu. Mimi wondered what building they lived in. She was still keeping track of the neighborhood from afar. Mimi introduced herself. The couple smiled but said nothing.

"You are from the neighborhood," said Mimi. "I've seen you around."

"Yes," was all Violette said.

Mimi was not satisfied. "Which building?"

"I used to be on the corner of Columbus, but I have moved to the country." Violette knew not to talk about the pied-à-terre.

"And you are Sabino, the sculptor."

"Si, soy yo," he said, raising his hand like an errant school-boy at roll call.

The inexplicable introduction of Spanish effectively brought the conversation to a halt.

"Well, enjoy your cheesecake," said Mimi, and she started to walk off.

"Can I make a suggestion?" said Violette.

"Well, sure."

"Did you ever think of an old-fashioned soda fountain? You know, root beer floats and things like that."

"An old-fashioned soda fountain. What a great idea. I wonder if I could find one."

Violette could tell that she was missing the point.

In reality, although Mimi liked the idea of antique equipment, nothing could have been more alien to her plans than a soda fountain. In her brain, in her roiling angry heart, was the idea of vengeance. Cato's was to undo Mykonos, steal their customers, steal their lightning, be the poster child of the new neighborhood, leaving the Greeks behind and looking a bit old-fashioned. Already she had established that she had "the real Cato's cheesecake." No one even remembered that the idea had started with Mykonos.

The next step, sorry, lovely Violette, would not be a soda fountain. Mimi didn't trust this Violette, who was on the arm of this attractive sculptor Sabino with hands like a car mechanic's that looked like they could fix anything. Mimi should be with Sabino. She wasn't too old for him. She was sixty-eight but everyone knew Violette was already seventy. Everyone also knew that she was married to a famous and attractive painter, even if Ruth said he did "girlie pictures"—and here was the girlie. Mimi had seen her husband in the neighborhood. This Violette had both of them? And she had a farm and an apartment somewhere on the block? She was greedy. She had two homes, two artist lovers, now she wanted a soda fountain. She wanted to have everything. And she was getting it. Greed was taking over.

No, Violette would not get her soda fountain. Mimi was about to receive her wine and liquor license. She would offer light and pleasant wines—Alsatian Riesling, Gewürztraminer, rosé from Provence, several high-quality but little-known champagnes served in crystal flutes. The menu was kept light to not upstage the desserts. There were hors d'oeuvres on Gerta's fluffy puff pastry. There was always a soup—cold soups for summer such as vichyssoise and hot for the colder seasons such as Parisian onion soup. She would stay open late and hope drunken people would come by for onion soup like she'd once heard they used to do in France. Onion soup and cheesecake. She would also offer a vegetable plate with a saffron-scented mayonnaise. Some days there was roasted marrow bone (Cato's favorite) and sometimes grilled trout. This was getting to be too much for just Mimi and Gerta.

Ruth thought Mimi could hire Lazarus, who she happened to know had previously been a pastry maker. But when approached, he said, "Get off the street and start it all over again? No thanks." Finally Mimi was able to hire the son of one of Ti Auguste's friends who was an accomplished line cook. This brought in the Haitians, Ti Auguste, and his lively friends for afternoon rosé.

Apparently Amy Artina from the *Times* had made it there, though no one had seen her. Ruth insisted that she had been disguised as the fat politician from New Jersey, since he hadn't looked quite right. But no one but Ruth thought he was Amy. The *Times* review began, "Cato's Café, on the Upper West Side, unlike Cato himself, avoids being ponderously Roman." Many thought this was an inside joke for classicists but Mimi and the Katsikases were certain this was a dig at Mykonos. Had she been back and not liked it? The review went on to praise the wine, the food, the ambience, the music. Amy did not even include her one obligatory cut. All praise. And she ended by writing that the cheesecake was "a welcome update on the Cato concept." She said it was "beyond exquisite." "Beyond exquisite" was her rarely used pet phrase. Some may have thought this was a slight against Cato himself, but others knew exactly whose cheesecake she was attacking.

Mimi had to admit that everything was effortlessly falling in line, like chessmen arranged on a magnetic board. Just hover the pawn, release, and it pops into place. That was how it had been going for Mimi. But every now and then she would catch herself thinking that A. G. Hoffman had more courage than she.

· · ·

Sometimes the gods align things perfectly. Ruth was walking down the street with her rolled-up copy of the *Times* when she saw Art. He had read the review before Ruth got her paper. He had shown it to Niki and said, "I have some

terrible news." Niki, in an agitated voice, replied, "The raccoons are back?"

Now Ruth gently poked Art with the roll and said, "You
see, you can drive the landsleit out, but they will come back
to bite you." Though this was Ruth's moment, Art was not
entirely paying attention. He was nervously looking down the
street at Rosita. It was Tuesday and he was almost sure his
spot was good on a Tuesday, but you could never be sure when
Rosita had her pad in hand.

Art did not know what Ruth was saying anyway. Later, he
spent more than an hour at his keyboard trying to figure out
what or who the "lambslite" were. He didn't know. Did it have
to do with city inspectors? Was it a reference to sheep, or
maybe goats? He should ask Adara. She was in the restaurant in
the kitchen as he began to explain his dilemma to her. But she
wasn't listening—did not even know he was talking to her.
She had her new headphones on and was listening to Greek
music, and worse, was singing along, a somber expression on
her face underscored by her dark eyebrows. She sang well.

Art gave up. But he was going to find these lambslite and
evict all of them. Raise their rents. Drive them *all* out this
time. They weren't going to bite him. But it seemed he
couldn't get at crazy Mrs. Landau—he already had and she
was somehow back. Why was she back? Was this what that
bag lady had meant? He couldn't get that cook, Gerta, because
she and her husband owned their own brownstone. They even
rented an apartment out of it. It was possible he could get the
Haitian cook. Yes. Maybe Lazarus had been right not to take
this job.

But Art realized that he didn't like what real estate had
done to him. When he'd started buying buildings, he'd

imagined himself becoming an elegant man of wealth, a leading citizen. It was the Jews. He had wanted a Jewish neighborhood because he thought they understood wealth. But they had fought him. Every Jew had at least two relatives who were lawyers. Of course there were the other Jewish landlords that he could work with, but they were competitors.

And there was that Violette. She wasn't Jewish. What was she? French? Yes, the French were more trouble than the Jews. Look how nice he had been to her, and how had she treated him? He tugged at the few strands of hair left on the top of his head. Violette seemed to like men with good hair. Her husband had good hair. And now she'd been seen around with this Sabino, who had thick dark hair, too. But why did Sabino always wear that flat wool hat? Was he covering something up? Maybe Art should find a hat. With a hat you get the benefit of the doubt.

In fact, Art was somewhat misjudging Violette. True, she liked Guy's hair and she liked Sabino's even better. But she didn't mind Art's baldness. Every time she looked at his shiny crown, she fondly remembered the sight of the delicate spangled fritillary posed on the top. Art knew nothing of this. He was certain women didn't like bald men. Niki, with his thick hair, whom women adored, assured his brother that this was not true. Laurette, the fleshy strawberry-blonde accountant Art had hired and whom he eventually started dating (great ample body but, at thirty-five, too young to have what he called "womanliness"), had the habit of patting the top of his head. This was supposed to be a gesture of affection, but Art could not help wondering if she was laughing at his baldness. Only Serafina adoringly kissed his barren shining top. But she was a professional. She knew what she was doing. None of the amateurs did that. He decided to shave his head—that was how bald people became stylish—but total baldness emphasized his extremely large ears and his pointed nose. Art had never realized that he had such big ears, but now he resembled an elephant. Elephants are not hip.

He could bribe the health authorities to get Cato's. But he knew he should not get too involved with those people because of Adara's dubious relationship with pasteurization. In fact, he'd had to bribe them to keep Mykonos open. Crazy Mrs. Landau could have turned the health department on *them*, but she was too dumb to think of it. Instead, she used the *New York Times*.

. . .

Violette did not go to Cato's often. She spent time on the farm with Guy. When she was in town, she was with Sabino in the pied-à-terre, where he was littering the floor with clay and steel. There were many bent and welded steel models for larger pieces, but the primary work was box-like and large, being shaped in clay to then be cast into bronze. Sabino's great gift was an ability to express emotion from geometric blocks. Once they were cast in bronze, they became irrefutable. Bronze is irrefutable. Marble tries to be pretty so it cannot be trusted. Steel sculptures look like buildings. Bronzes look like mountains. Violette had to be bronze. The warmth and sensuality of Violette could be expressed in bronze but never captured with steel. But you could not work with bronze on your own, and Sabino liked to be on his own. If only someone could get him to take his work to the foundry. He had a number of clay pieces ready to cast, but bronze was made from copper and the price of copper was high. He could wait. Sabino had no deadlines.

When Sabino was alone, he often went to Cato's for a cheesecake and an espresso, and one peaceful afternoon Mimi got into a discussion with him about the cake. To her surprise, he knew the original recipe and wondered where Mimi's ideas had come from. She said it was an "interpretation."

"I thought it was supposed to be burned as a sacrifice. But it wouldn't burn."

"Why would you sacrifice a cheesecake?" She was looking at his robust hands.

While they spoke, Mimi was forming an idea. A big one. One of her best. The coup de grâce for the Greeks. A Sabino Begotxu original on the sidewalk in front of her café.

Normally it would take a great deal of money to acquire a large public sculpture from an artist as well known as Sabino. Luckily Sabino did not believe in exchanging his work for money—but there was another problem. He also did not believe in displaying it. His reputation rested on that one award-winning work in Buenos Aires that had made him famous before it became known how difficult he was. No museums had managed to acquire him. His work had once been included in a temporary exhibition of contemporary sculptures at the Tate in London. One had stood in the square of a seldom-visited Flemish town and another still was displayed in his hometown of San Sebastián, near the ocean. It was in all the guidebooks as something to see in town along with the Chillidas. Ocean spray had eroded the metal, which Sabino said was part of the concept. He had titled it *Zaborra*, which is Basque for "trash." His work always had cryptic titles.

Sabino told Mimi that he had been working on a nine-foot statue of Violette, which Violette liked and wanted him to place somewhere. "But I'm not going to do that," he'd replied. Violette had taken it to the foundry in Brooklyn herself and had it cast in bronze at no small expense. Mimi really didn't want a statue of Violette at her café. But the only Begotxu in North America? Everyone would come. Mimi had to acquire it, and she knew how. The price was root beer.

It worked. Once she'd secured an old-fashioned fountain, she lured Violette in during her one or two afternoons a week in the city. Mimi took the opportunity to befriend her. In time, she nudged Violette into telling her more about Sabino's sculpture, and with more time they became coconspirators. Violette said she would like to see the piece on Mimi's sidewalk. One day she offered to take Mimi over to the "studio" (a better word than "pied-à-terre") to see the piece later that night.

. . .

Ruth was walking down West Eighty-Sixth Street with her Zabar's bag. She wasn't using a cane anymore. "Too bad," she thought when she heard a voice behind her shouting her name. She knew it was Linda. She wanted to run, but she still knew people on Eighty-Sixth Street and she would look ridiculous running with Linda chasing behind her. Besides, Linda probably ran faster. So Ruth stopped, sighed heavily, and waited.

Linda, in near hysterics, shouted, "You have to stop them!"

It turned out Linda was talking about Mimi, who was soon to be on her way to "Sabino and Violette's place," a label only used by Linda, to see the sculpture. "If Mimi goes over there she will find out that Guy and Violette rented her old apartment, and maybe even how they got it," said Linda, intimating at gossip that she alone knew. "Mimi will be so mad, she'll never take the statue."

And so Linda's plot unfolded. (The purpose of all of Linda's plots was to keep herself at the center.) Rushing, Ruth and Linda managed to beat Mimi to her old apartment and saw the sad sight of the bare walls and empty rooms cluttered with Sabino's work scraps on the floor. They convinced Sabino to move the sculpture on its large dolly down to Linda's apartment on a lower floor before Mimi arrived.

As they were rushing to move the piece, Linda was busy making calls. She was urgently trying to arrange for television coverage of the sculpture's public unveiling once they got it down to Cato's, but producers were only interested in sending their crew after the piece was installed. When she got Saul on the phone, he told her he'd really love to cover the unveiling but couldn't make it. In reality, he didn't want to get trapped talking to Linda.

Instead, Linda called the videographer who had done Masha's bat mitzvah. He rushed over to capture the process from the start. She instructed him that since this was her apartment, he had to make sure to get some good shots of her, "including good close-ups." Linda bitterly pointed out that he had "completely missed" her at the bat mitzvah. She had bought a bright coral-colored dress for the occasion, the kind of clothing she had never been seen in before, because she had thought it would make her look "artsy."

. . .

It was explained to Mimi that Sabino's studio was too far away and for convenience they had moved the piece to Linda's apartment. This would have aroused suspicion in someone who did not know Linda. After all, how far away could Sabino's studio be? But Mimi recognized Linda's conspiracy to put her apartment, and therefore herself, at the center of the action. Why should Mimi care?

When Mimi first entered the building, her building, to see the sculpture, she became a juvenile delinquent contemplating how best to deface the lobby. She enjoyed this flirtation with childishness the same way that Violette liked her root beer floats. In recent weeks, Mimi had been overcome with impulses that her friends found disturbing but she found refreshing. Ruth enjoyed them too, though, and confessed that she had "smacked the Greek" with the *New York Times*. They had posted the *Times* review on the window of Cato's Café, and Mimi was planning to order a sign with an enlarged quote to put by the entrance:

AVOIDS BEING PONDEROUSLY ROMAN
—*THE NEW YORK TIMES*

But Gerta argued that it would be more effective to post the quote about the cheesecake being "beyond exquisite." That was what the café was famous for, and, of course, it was Gerta who made the cheesecake.

. . .

As Mimi entered Linda's apartment, a unit she had never visited when she lived in the building, she thought the sculpture, with its black patina—black as a truffle—was magnificent: three cubes stacked at odd angles with a 45-degree trapezoidal block on top. Mimi couldn't explain it, but it really looked like Violette. There was something trapezoidal about her. Violette tilted her head obligingly. They should simply call it "Violette," Mimi announced, a good Begotxu title.

Sabino flipped his wool beret over the videographer's camera. (By the way, it did expose a thick top of black hair.)

He and Violette whispered to Mimi, "We cannot call it 'Violette.'"

"Why not?"

"It will hurt my husband," said Violette softly. Linda's ears perked up the way a German shepherd's do. Now they were going to get into a good story.

"He has been very understanding, but this would be too much. 'Violette' was his work. It would seem like we were laughing at his painting.

"Besides," said Violette, offering one argument too many, "it will make the landlord really angry."

"Landlord" was a code word that got Mimi going. Who was their landlord? Where did they live? Now Mimi was interested.

"It doesn't matter. I just have a difficult landlord. Very emotional."

Mimi relaxed a bit. This wasn't the Greek. He was heartless and without emotions.

"So then what do you call the sculpture?" asked Mimi, who didn't truly want it to be called "Violette" either (although if she'd known how it would drive Art to madness, she might have been tempted).

"You have to call it something. You always name your pieces," Mimi insisted.

They looked to Sabino and the videographer, who were now back in the main room getting a close-up.

Sabino softly suggested, "Cato."

Cheesecake Recipes: A History

This novel takes place on West Eighty-Sixth Street between Columbus and Amsterdam Avenues. Though the Upper West Side was once famous for bakeries and especially cheesecake, there are few bakeries left now. The only quality cheesecake still being sold close to the setting of this novel is around the corner on Eighty-Sixth and Amsterdam, at Barney Greengrass. Greengrass started the restaurant in Harlem in 1908. In 1929 he moved it to Eighty-Sixth Street, where it still has its original art deco cabinets and shelves. His grandson Gary Greengrass gave me these ingredients for their classic New York cheesecake:

Graham cracker crust
Graham crackers
Sugar
Melted butter

Cheesecake

3 pounds 12 ounces cream cheese

6 ounces corn starch

2½ eggs

4 ounces heavy cream

Vanilla to taste (1 or 2 teaspoons)

New York cheesecake, according to New York legend, was invented in 1929 by Arnold Reuben. Reuben, a German Jew, owned delis that were famous for their sandwiches named after celebrities. (But the Reuben sandwich was not his creation.) His cheesecake was created for his restaurant on West Eighty-Second Street and Broadway. Therefore, New York cheesecake is an Upper West Side invention first made four blocks from the location of this novel.

There was cheesecake in New York before Reuben, often made from Central European recipes, but it did not use cream cheese. My Lithuanian-born grandmother, who grew up on the Lower East Side before the Reuben invention, made cheesecake without the graham cracker crust and with farmer's cheese, not cream cheese. It was lemony, lighter, and less dense.

Farmer's cheese, which is essential for Eastern European cheesecake, can be bought or made. To make it, heat a gallon of milk to a simmer and, just before a full boil, slowly stir in about a half cup of white vinegar. After it curdles, pour into a strainer lined with cheesecloth and drain off the whey. Squeeze out the rest of the liquid, form the farmer's cheese into a ball, and refrigerate.

The cream cheese itself was also a New York invention. William Lawrence of Chester, New York, tried to copy

Neufchâtel, a French cheese dating to the Middle Ages, at the request of a New York City grocery store in search of a richer fresh cheese. In 1875 he created cream cheese, which itself became a New York City specialty.

Reuben also added the graham cracker crust, which had been invented only a few years earlier by celebrated Los Angeles pie maker Monroe Boston Strause. Strause had become famous for inventing the chiffon pie, for which the first graham cracker crust was created—but it was Reuben who made it standard for New York cheesecake.

Reuben's recipe

Crust

1½ cups (about 21 squares) graham cracker crumbs

5 tablespoons butter

1 teaspoon honey

¼ cup granulated sugar

Filling

5 packages (8 ounces each) cream cheese, at room temperature

2 tablespoons all-purpose flour

1 tablespoon confectioners' sugar

1½ cups granulated sugar

Grated rind of 1 lemon

½ teaspoon orange liqueur

¾ teaspoon vanilla extract

2 egg yolks, at room temperature

5 eggs, at room temperature

Preparation

1. Preheat oven to 400 degrees F. Heavily coat 10-inch springform pan with cooking spray.
2. Prepare crust. Mix graham cracker crumbs, butter, honey and sugar together with hands until well blended and crumbs appear moist. Pour into springform pan. With hands, spread evenly across the bottom and pat down firmly.
3. Place cream cheese, flour, confectioners' sugar, sugar, and lemon rind in a large mixing bowl and beat on high until they are completely blended. Add orange liqueur, vanilla and 2 yolks, and beat again. Add eggs one at a time, beating well after each addition. Pour into prepared springform pan. Batter will fill pan.
4. Bake for 10 minutes. Top will be golden. Lower oven temperature to 200 degrees and bake for 35 to 45 minutes or until top browns, cake feels bouncy to the touch, and a toothpick tests clean. Remove from oven and let cool to room temperature.
5. Serve immediately or cover and refrigerate. Bring to room temperature before serving.

Ratner's was a kosher dairy restaurant founded in 1905, with a location on Delancey Street. A second restaurant, on Second Avenue, was open all night, which was popular with celebrities when the Yiddish theater was in the neighborhood. Ratner's was also popular with politicians. Nelson Rockefeller, then governor of New York, always went to Ratner's on the eve of an election because he believed it brought him good luck. Robert Kennedy, who famously had a childlike love of sweets, despite his trim build, was a fan of

Ratner's as well. (I met him when I worked on his campaign in the 1968 Indiana primary and personally witnessed him merrily devouring a bowl of vanilla ice cream.) Ratner's did not close until 2004, and while their cheesecake was famous and their restaurant was older than Reuben's, they are not credited with being first. Their cheesecake uses both farmer's cheese and cream cheese and has a lighter, more interesting texture than Reuben's. Nor does it use a graham cracker crust.

This is the recipe from their 1975 cookbook:

Dough
Can be prepared in advance. Makes enough for two cakes. Can be frozen or used to make cookies—see recipe below.

1 cup sugar
1 teaspoon vanilla extract
1 cup shortening
1 teaspoon lemon extract
1 cup butter
2 eggs
3 cups sifted cake flour
½ teaspoon salt
2 cups all-purpose flour
1 teaspoon baking powder
In a bowl, combine all ingredients with hands.
Refrigerate 3 to 4 hours, or preferably overnight.

Filling (for ½ the dough recipe)
1 lb. cream cheese (room temp)

3 tbsp. all-purpose flour
1 lb. farmer's cheese
4 eggs
1.3 cups sugar
6 tbsp. soft butter
1.5 cups sour cream
2 tsp. vanilla extract

1. Preheat oven to 350.
2. Press enough dough into ungreased 9 x 13 x 2-inch (22.5 x 32.5 x 5-cm.) baking pan to form a thin layer over the bottom and sides.
3. Cream the butter and sugar, add cheeses, and continue to cream.
4. Add the rest of the ingredients and mix (slowly in mixer or by hand) till smooth.
5. Pour filling into pan and bake for around 1 hour.

Ratner's popularized the strawberry cheesecake. This was their topping.

½ cup strawberry jam
1 pint whole strawberries, hulled
½ cup apple jelly, heated

1. When cake is cool spread jam over top and stud with fresh strawberries.
2. Glaze with melted apple jelly.

But Reuben's recipe dominated, and soon New York cheesecake was entirely cream cheese–based. Nothing could be more New York.

It became a local obsession. Hollywood laughed about it in the 1942 comedy *All Through the Night*. When gangster Humphrey Bogart is not served his favorite version of cheesecake, he menacingly tells the waiter, "When I order cheesecake, I don't expect to get mucilage!" So begins a hunt for his missing cheesecake maker that leads to a ring of Nazi spies—a New York story.

. . .

The Upper West Side was a bakery neighborhood. Four celebrated bake shops were on West Seventy-Second Street alone: Cake Masters, Bloom's, Café Éclair, and the Royale Pastry Shop. Cushman's, Party Cake, and Grossinger's were also in the neighborhood. An Upper West Sider once had a lot of choices for cheesecake.

Opened in 1939 by Alexander Selinger, a sugar broker from Vienna, the Éclair was a center of Upper West Side Jewish culture. But it eventually changed hands and after a bankruptcy filing in 1996, the café's contents were auctioned off and the site became a Krispy Kreme donut shop.

In 1981, Grossinger's—the very one from my novel— opened a second shop on West Eighty-Eighth and Columbus. Their cheesecake was very similar to Reuben's, with a graham cracker crust and a cream cheese base, but was made richer with more egg yolks and lighter without flour or cornstarch.

Grossinger's cheesecake recipe
Yields two 10-inch cheesecakes or four 8-inch cheesecakes
To make the base:
1½ cups graham cracker crumbs

1 cup granulated sugar
1½ sticks melted butter
Mix together in the mixing machine.

For the cheesecake:
1 pound of sifted powdered sugar (10x)
½ pound butter
3 tbsp vanilla
3½ pounds of cream cheese
5 eggs plus 5 yolks (should equal ½ quart)
2 cups sour cream

Grease either a 10-inch pan (or springform) with a
2-inch height or three 8-inch pans with 2-inch height
(or springforms).

Mix the graham cracker base ingredients and line
the bottom and sides by pressing it in with your hands.

Cream the butter and powdered sugar with vanilla
in a mixing machine until smooth. Then add cream
cheese and mix again. Next, add the eggs and yolks and
mix. Then add the sour cream and mix again. Next,
pour into pan over the graham cracker base almost to
the top. Then put the filled pans into a water bath (a
large square aluminum container) filled halfway with
water. Place it in the oven. Bake at 360 degrees for
about 1 hour 15 minutes, until firm. Then, take it out,
pour out the water, and let it cool in the round pans.

Sometimes, before baking their cheesecakes Grossinger's
would gently stir in melted dark chocolate to make a marble
version, or they would add toasted chopped hazelnuts or

pumpkin puree. "You can add anything to a cheesecake," said Herb Grosinger. (Herb's name and the store have different spellings because their family is a convergence of two different families with the same name but different spelling.) In 1991, Grossinger's lost the lease on their Seventy-Sixth Street store because their landlord closed five shops to make way for a large high-rent Gap store. The Eighty-Eighth Street store closed in 1999 when Herb Grosinger said he was not able to pay after the rent hike. He now has no shop but still ships cakes to order.

. . .

Sylvia Balser Hirsch opened a bakery on Columbus Avenue in 1968. Her cheesecake had been a star attraction in her husband's failed barbeque restaurant and now it would be the centerpiece of her new bakery, Miss Grimble's. There was no such person. Sylvia just liked the name. By 1971 she claimed to be selling 2,200 cheesecakes a month. Her vanilla cheesecake was the most popular, but she made twenty different flavors including macaroon rum raisin cheesecake, coffee rum cheesecake, Cointreau cheesecake, chocolate cheesecake, chocolate walnut cheesecake, chocolate orange marble cheesecake, and even a savory cheesecake with cream cheese and Roquefort. But in 1988 she sold the shop to a company in the Bronx.

Here is her recipe for Miss Grimble's Caramel Pecan Cheesecake.

Crust

2 cups honey graham cracker crumbs

2 tablespoons sugar

6 tablespoons butter or margarine, melted

Blend the crumbs with the sugar and butter or margarine. Press onto the bottom and sides of a ten-inch springform.

Filling
3 eight-ounce packages cream cheese
4 eggs
2 cups dark brown sugar, packed
1½ teaspoons instant powdered coffee
1 tablespoon vanilla
⅛ teaspoon salt
½ cup chopped pecans
Chopped pecans for garnish
Butter

Preheat oven to 350 degrees F.

In an electric mixer cream the cheese with the eggs and sugar. Add the instant coffee, vanilla, salt, and pecans, and mix on medium speed until well blended. Pour into prepared springform and bake in preheated oven for 40 to 50 minutes. Cool to room temperature, then chill. To serve, top with additional chopped pecans that have been lightly tossed in butter.

Louis Lichtman, a Hungarian, established Lichtman's on Eighty-Fifth and Amsterdam in 1947. In 1962 he moved the shop to the southwest corner of Eighty-Sixth and Amsterdam. After forty years in business, he closed and moved to New Jersey when, he claimed, the landlord raised the rent

500 percent. "There won't be any more bakeries like this one," said Herb Grosinger.

. . .

There are a few cheesecake makers still in the neighborhood and even some new ideas. Tavern on the Green, in Central Park at Sixty-Seventh Street, offers a New York cheesecake. Sometimes they make it gluten-free, which is a growing demand in New York food. All they had to do was develop a gluten-free recipe for the graham cracker crust, although a simpler solution would have been to follow some of the old-time recipes that have no crust at all.

Café Lalo opened in the neighborhood in 1988 and closed in 2023 after a lengthy dispute with the landlord. Included on their long menu were twenty-four cheesecakes:

Amaretto Cheesecake (Kosher)
Apple Crumb Cheesecake
Bailey's Coffee Cheesecake (Kosher)
Black & White Cheesecake (Kosher)
Black Forest Cheesecake
Blueberry Cheesecake
Brownie Cheesecake
Cherry Cheesecake
Chocolate Oreo Cheesecake (Kosher)
Dulce de Leche Cheesecake (Kosher)
Italian Cheesecake
Key Lime Cheesecake
Maple Walnut Cheesecake (Kosher)

Mint Chocolate Cheesecake (Kosher)
Mississippi Mud Cheesecake
Nutella Cheesecake
Old Fashioned Classic Cheesecake (Kosher)
Peanut Butter Cheesecake
Raspberry Almond Cheesecake
Red Velvet Cheesecake (Kosher)
Salty Caramel Cheesecake (Kosher)
Snickers Bar Cheesecake (Kosher)
Strawberry Cheesecake
Sugarless Cheesecake

As Herb Grosinger said, you can add anything to a cheesecake.

The Last Hungarians

Today, bakeries are hard to find in the neighborhood and the Hungarians have disappeared. The closest Hungarian bakery is the Hungarian Pastry Shop all the way up Amsterdam at 111th Street in Morningside Heights. It was founded by a Hungarian couple in 1961. In 1976, they sold out to a Greek couple, Peter and Wendy Binioris. Peter and Wendy were not like the Katsikases. They kept the Hungarian recipes and the cozy feel of a family-run café. Since 2012, the café has been run by their son, Philip Binioris.

They're known not for cheesecake but for strudel, and their cherry cheese strudel resembles Mimi's version of Cato's cheesecake in my novel. The filling is similar to a classic New York cheesecake such as Barney Greengrass's. This is Philip's description of how to make cherry cheese strudel:

Strudel is a fairly easy pastry to make, unless you are making your own dough, in which case it is fairly complicated.

A proper strudel dough is composed of flour, water, and salt, and requires a large, perfectly flat surface and a lot of patience. It should be tissue paper thin.

To make the strudel, stack two sheets of dough and brush with melted butter and sprinkle with sweet fine breadcrumbs.

Add two more sheets and repeat with butter and breadcrumbs. On the short end of the sheet, spread out your filling (in this case a mix of cream cheese, sugar, eggs, cornstarch, vanilla, and sour cherries) and then roll up the strudel into a log and coat it in melted butter.

Bake at 375 F for 20 min, remove and brush with egg wash, rotate, and bake again for 15 min. (Baking times and temperature vary by oven.)

New York's First Cheesecake

Many would say the first cheesecake in New York was Jewish. But before the New York Jews and their cream cheese cheesecake, there was Sicilian cheesecake. And long before that, there was English cheesecake. Cheesecake was popular in eighteenth-century England.

Eliza Smith, whose 1727 *Compleat Housewife* was one of the most popular cookbooks of eighteenth-century England, wrote numerous cheesecake recipes. The book remained in print long after her death at an unknown date in the 1730s. A 1742 edition became the first cookbook published in the

American colonies. So it is likely that the first cheesecake eaten in New York was created by Eliza Smith. Smith began making most of her cheesecakes the way cheesemaking begins: by adding rennet, an enzyme from a calf's stomach lining, to milk to make it curdle.

Was the first New York cheesecake an almond cheesecake? This is one of her recipes from the sixteenth English edition in 1758. It requires fresh milk, and often such eighteenth-century recipes begin with the instruction to "milk a cow." Smith's book was well known in New York in the mid-eighteenth century and there were even city cows available for milking. Here is the recipe:

To make Cheesecakes

Take a pint of cream and warm it. And put to it five quarts of milk warm from the cow, then put rennet to it, and when it come [Note: curdles], put the curd in a linen bag or cloth and let it drain well from the whey, but do not squeeze too much; then put it in a mortar, and break the curd as fine as butter. Then put to your curd half a pound of almonds, blanched and beaten exceedingly finely (or half a pound of dry macaroons beaten very finely). If you have almonds, grate in a Naples biscuit [Note: a common ingredient in eighteenth-century baking, similar to a ladyfinger, made with whipped eggs, sugar and flour—light and dry]; but if you use macaroons, you need not; then add to it the yolks of nine eggs beaten; a whole nutmeg grated, two perfumed plumbs dissolved in rose or orange flower water [Note: sweet stewed plums], half a pound of fine sugar, and mix all well together. Then melt a pound and a quarter of butter and stir it well in, and half a pound of currents [sic], plumped (soaked). Let it stand to cool till you're ready to use it. Then make your puff-paste thus: take a pound of fine flour and wet it with cold water, roll it out, and put in it by degrees a pound of fresh butter; use it just as it is made. [Note: Presumably she meant "bake it" by "use it."]

Old York Cheesecake

In England, different regions had their own cheesecake styles. In Yorkshire, the tradition of making cakes with cheese curds goes back to the late Middle Ages. Today they're made with currants and rum. Then there are Wilfra cakes, made with apples and cured Wensleydale cheese. In Yorkshire's cathedral town of Ripon, the seventh-century Saint Wilfra is celebrated in August with a procession. The custom began in the twelfth century. Wilfra cakes were baked and placed along the route to treat the people walking in the procession. The custom of Wilfra cakes had been dying out, but the museum in Ripon has been trying to revive the custom, urging locals to bake them. They must be made with Wensleydale, the local Yorkshire cheese, which used to be made from sheep milk but is now usually made from cow milk. The museum claims there is an old Yorkshire saying: "Apple cake without some cheese is like a kiss without a squeeze."

This is the museum's Wilfra cake recipe:

Shortcrust pastry
8 oz plain flour

4 oz butter or margarine

1 tablespoon caster [Note: suggest granulated] sugar

A pinch of salt

1 egg yolk

1–2 teaspoons water

Filling

1.5 lb peeled and thinly sliced cooking apples

3 oz demerara sugar

3 oz grated Wensleydale cheese

Method

Rub the butter into the flour, sugar and salt. Mix to a stiff paste with the egg yolk and a little water. Leave to rest in a cool place until required.

Line a Swiss roll tin or pie tin with half the pastry and lightly prick the bottom. Lay on the finely sliced apples and cover with demerara sugar. Grate the cheese onto the top. Put on a pastry lid and brush with milk and sugar. Make a few slits along the top and bake for 10 minutes at 425° F; 220° C; Gas Mark 7 for 10 minutes and then lower to 350° F; 180° C; Gas Mark 4 for a further 30 minutes.

Serve with cream.

Scottish Cheesecake

Cheesecakes were enjoyed in Scotland, too. Mistress Margaret Dods included cheesecake recipes in her influential 1829 *Cook and Housewife's Manual*. Actually, there was no such person as Margaret Dods. The name was taken from a character in a Walter Scott novel. The real author was an early feminist, journalist, and novelist in Edinburgh, Christian Isobel Johnstone, who chose not to put her real name on what became her famous cookbook. She also declined to put her name on her numerous successful novels. She was the editor of a number of politically edgy newspapers and magazines but chose to maintain her privacy. She defines cheesecakes as various puddings, ingredients more or less rich, baked in paste. Some of her cheesecakes, such as lemon and orange, have no cheese. "Cheeseless" cheesecake was not uncommon at the time. Curdled milk was considered cheese (which, in fact, it is). She gave this recipe in her book:

> Mix with the dry beat curd of a quart and a half of milk, a half-pound of picked currants, white sugar to taste, and also pounded cinnamon, the beat yolks of four eggs, the peel of a lemon grated off on lumps of sugar used for sweetening, a half pint of scalded cream, and a glass of brandy. Mix the ingredients well and fill patty-pans lined with a thin light puff-pastry nearly full. Twenty minutes will bake them in a quick oven. They may be iced.

A Photo Finish

In 1850, a Frenchman named L. D. Blanquart made a major improvement in the new craft of photography. If the paper was coated with albumen, he discovered, its pores would be sealed and the paper could capture a much clearer image. Albumen was made by separating egg whites, adding salt, and beating to a froth. The albumen was kept for at least a week or more before being applied to paper, giving photography studios a strong sulfuric egg odor.

But there was another problem. What were they to do with the leftover yolks? Heinz K. Henisch and Bridget Ann Henisch, historians of late-nineteenth-century photography, found an article in the September 2, 1861, issue of the *British Journal of Photography* that answered:

> A HINT TO ALBUMINIZERS. What can you do with the yolks of your eggs? Make them into cheesecakes that will be pronounced unrivaled . . .

The idea caught on in the photography world. The Henisches were even able to find a recipe in *The British Journal Photographic Almanac* (1862) for that nineteenth-century cheeseless cheesecake.

THE PHOTOGRAPHER'S CHEESECAKE

To convert the yolks of eggs used for albumenizing to useful purposes: Dissolve a quarter pound of butter in a basin placed on a hob [Note: a shelf for warming at the side of a stove], stir in a quarter of a pound of pounded sugar, and beat well together: then add the yolks of three eggs that have been previously well-beaten; beat up all together thoroughly; throw in half a grated nutmeg and a pinch of salt; and lastly add the juice of two fine-flavoured lemons and the rind of one lemon that has been peeled very thin; beat all up together thoroughly, and pour into a dish lined with puff-paste, and bake for about twenty minutes. This is a most delicious dish.

Russian Pashka

In central and eastern Europe, cheesecake is made with farmer's cheese, a habit Jews from this part of Europe brought to New York. In Russia, the most celebrated of these cheesecakes is pashka. To make pashka requires a pashka mold, a wooden trapezoid with folkloric paintings decorating the outside. In czarist times, when the Orthodox Church forbade the eating of dairy during Lent, pashka was the star of the Easter feast. Rural people even took pashka to church for the midnight service on Easter Eve to usher it in at the earliest moment. Traditionally the Lenten fast was broken by eating foods that had been blessed. The pashka had been blessed and was ready for the event. Elena Molokhovets, the leading chronicler of aristocratic cuisine in czarist Russia, offered several recipes for pashka, some with fresh fruit. This is her recipe for pashka tsarskaja, or royal pashka, translated by Joyce Toomre:

> Place in a saucepan 5 pounds finely sieved farmer's cheese, 10 raw eggs, 1 lb. very fresh unsalted butter, and 2 lbs very fresh sour cream. Set on top of the stove, stirring constantly with a wooden spatula so that the mixture does not burn. As soon as the cheese begins to boil—that is, as soon as even one bubble appears—immediately remove from the fire, set on ice, and stir until it is completely cool. Add 1–2 lbs sugar ground with 1 vanilla bean, about ½ glass blanched ground almonds, and ½ glass currants. Mix everything thoroughly, pile into a large mold lined with a napkin, and add weights. After 24 hours carefully unmold on to a plate.

Alsatian Cheesecake

The French are not big cheesecake fans—except in eastern France, with its German influence. In Alsace, cheesecake is made with fromage blanc, a ubiquitous French product. It resembles sour cream and is made by using bacteria to curdle milk.

This recipe from 1979 is by Pierre Gaertner, the chef of a celebrated restaurant in the Alsatian town of Ammerschwihr, Aux Armes de France. It is a summer dessert, popular in the Vosges mountains along the German border.

300 grams pâte brisée [a dough made by working
butter into flour with egg yolks]

300 grams fromage blanc
150 grams powdered sugar
1 teaspoon vanilla sugar
4 eggs
3 tablespoons crème fraîche
zest of a half lemon
100 grams raisins
1 small glass kirsch

Work the pâte brisée into a buttered pie dish or
springform.

Soak the raisins in the kirsch.

Mix the fromage blanc with the crème fraîche in a
bowl. Add the egg yolks, powdered sugar, vanilla
sugar, and lemon zest and mix well until it is the
texture of a mousse.

Whip the egg whites until fluffy and fold carefully into the mixture.

Pour mixture onto pastry. Add the raisins.

Bake in a moderate oven for 35 or forty minutes.

The Big Cheese

In Sicily, the word for cheesecake is "cassata," and a cassata is always made with ricotta cheese. Like pashka in Russia, it is the cake used to celebrate Easter. In earlier centuries it was made by nuns in convents for Easter but also by Jews to celebrate Purim.

Some say the word "cassata" comes from the Latin word for cheese. But others argue for an Arabic origin, from "qas'ah," for the inwardly sloped pie mold used to make a cassata. Certainly such a sweet dish would not have been possible if the Arabs hadn't introduced sugar to Europe. There is no sugar in Cato's recipe because he had no knowledge of sugar.

There are two versions of cassata: a baked one and one in which ingredients are simply pressed in the mold and refrigerated together. The most common version is sponge cake filled with sweetened ricotta cheese, candied orange peel, and chips of dark chocolate, all wrapped in green marzipan and decorated with candied fruit. Sometimes the marzipan is striped. The point is that cassata is for celebration and should look joyous. Ferrara pastry shop in Manhattan's Little Italy, run by the same family since 1892, was making cassata long before Reuben was making his cheesecake. Ferrara also claims to have introduced espresso to America.

This 1971 recipe comes from Pino Correnti's book, *Il libro d'oro della cucina e dei vini di sicilia*. It is one of several cassata recipes in the book that attempts to define Sicilian cooking. Here is the recipe for home use:

Push half a kilo of very fresh ricotta through a sieve. With a wooden spoon, mix in three grams of confectioner's sugar, a pinch of vanilla, and a little sweet liqueur or rum. Work it until you obtain a soft cream. Enrich it with pieces of chocolate and diced candied fruit. Meanwhile, line the walls and bottom of a round mold with a diameter of approximately fifteen centimeters with white pastry paper and cover with 550 grams of sponge cake cut into slices, using a little cream to make them adhere to the paper.

Pour the ricotta cream into the mold and level it with a spatula.

Now close with a final layer of sponge cake and place the mold back in the refrigerator so that the cream solidifies. If we want to embolden the mixture, when we work the ricotta cream we will use different colors and divide it into three portions and pour in various sweet liqueurs of different colors.

Then carry out the operation of filling the carefully prepared mold, smoothing the three different levels, separated by slices of sponge cake. Cover it with a plate and turn it over. Now the cassata is ready to be covered with green pistachio marzipan, to then be adorned as tradition dictates with candied fruit— pumpkin with long and thin curved strips, wafers of rose buds, chips of silver coated chocolate, orange peels in the elegant curves that before being Baroque were Sicilian.

Pino Correnti also offered other cassatas—one from Palermo and one from Erice. He mentions the one from Ferrara in New York. Ferrara, whose advertising slogan is "There is no such thing as too much cheesecake," sometimes caters events. In the 1970s they were making cassatas so large that they could not be transported. They would transport the cake, filling, marzipan, and garnishes and, with engineering acumen, construct the cassata at the venue. The cake would have seven or eight tiers and stand, with all its elaborate Sicilian decoration in candied fruit, at least six feet high, sometimes taller. An estimated seventy pounds of ricotta cheese would be used.

Greeks Bearing Cheesecake

The fictitious Adara Katsikas in this novel is not the only Greek to insist that Greeks invented cheesecake earlier than Cato. Greek documents from the fifth century BCE mention cakes made of honey and fresh cheese on the island of Samos off the coast of Turkey. Still, while the Greeks wrote about many things, they didn't write recipes, so Cato's is the first recipe we have. Centuries after Cato, in the second century AD, Athenaeus describes a cheesecake from the third century BCE made by brides for their weddings. He claims that Callimachus, a poet and literary authority born in 310 BCE, knew this cake from an earlier written work on cheesecakes. Unfortunately this work has not been found, but Athenaeus, centuries later, gave a simple recipe for beaten cheese and honey with flour.

Melopita, which literally means "honey pie," is similar to the ancient cheesecake. It comes from the island of Sifnos, which, like the Katsikases' island, is in the Cyclades chain. Melopita is usually prepared with local fresh cheese, myzithra, which is made from goat or sheep milk. Sometimes melopita is made with anthotyros, another fresh cheese. This cheese has a tartness that ricotta lacks and interacts well with the sweetness of honey. You will see American recipes for melopita calling for ricotta cheese or, even worse, cottage cheese. Like Sicilian cassata and Russian pashka, it is traditional for Easter.

The most highly regarded Greek food writer of the mid-twentieth century was Nicholas Tselementes, who happened to come from the isle of Sifnos. Here is his recipe for melopita:

2 pounds myzithra
1 pound honey
10 ounces sugar
8 eggs
2 tablespoons powdered cinnamon
12 ounces flour
a little butter and salt

Mix myzithra with sugar in a large bowl. Add honey and mix. Beat eggs well and add them to the cheese mixture and work thoroughly. Prepare a pastry dough with flour, a little butter, and salt. Make a pie crust and line the bottom of baking pan. Spread filling on it and bake in a moderate oven for 30 to 35 minutes until golden brown. When done, spread all over with cinnamon, cool, and cut in square pieces or diamond shapes.

New York Cheesecake Goes Global

Like Kentucky Fried Chicken and pizza, cheesecake has become a sign of a modern developed society. Decades after Arnold Reuben, New York cheesecake became famous around the United States. Still, it was believed that if you wanted a real New York cheesecake, you either had to go to New York or have one shipped from there. But by the end of the twentieth century, New York cheesecake had imitators around the world, part of a growing trend for international cuisine.

This was how New York cheesecake became a famous Basque dish, "the Basque cheesecake." The restaurant La Viña, founded in 1959, is a small bar restaurant in the old section of San Sebastián. It specializes in traditional Basque food, especially from the Gipuzkoa region, such as salt cod–stuffed pepper, spider crab, and squid in ink. The bar was popular for its pintxos, Basque bar snacks.

Santiago Rivera, whose parents had started La Viña, represented a new generation. Francisco Franco, who ruled Spain for thirty-six years, had made Spain an international pariah and under his rule few foreign products were available. After the dictator's death in 1975, Spain began to open up, and by the 1980s it was fashionable to use foreign products. In between his traditional dishes, Santi was able to begin experimenting with a foreign idea: New York cheesecake.

In the rich tradition of Basque cuisine, there had never been cheesecake of any kind. The closest thing was a yogurt cake with huckleberries or cuajada, curdled goat or sheep milk served like a pudding with cherry preserves. If Santi had wanted to create a Basque cheesecake, he could have started with fresh curds of Basque cheese. The Basques have a strong cheese-making tradition, mostly with sheep milk but also goat and cow. But Santi had a foreign, not a Basque, idea. Like a New York cheesecake, his would be made from cream cheese, a typically New York product that had never been used in Basque cooking. (Today there is a Spanish-made cream cheese, which is somewhat saltier. He sometimes uses that but prefers the American for an authentic taste.)

His was a slight variation on New York's. There was no crust, which sometimes is seen in New York also. But rather than gently baking on a low heat, he used a very hot oven and baked it quickly so it formed its own kind of crust, darkened, nearly burned on the top, and removed it from the oven while the center was still creamy like a custard. Santi slipped his creation onto the menu and found that his customers liked it. Nigella Lawson, the British television food star, liked it too, and once she talked about it, it spread to social media. Now Santi's Basque cheesecake is known all over the world. It's particularly popular in Turkey, which only had a tradition of savory cheese pastry—not made with cream cheese—called "borekas."

I am not sure how well the recipe is carried out in other places. I was in a small fishing town in Maine, eating cheeseburgers and beer with a local lobsterman, when the waitress presented a dessert menu. To my amazement, there it was: "Basque cheesecake." Of course I ordered it, but I found that they did not bake it at a hot enough temperature and it had no crust or creamy center, so it seemed like an unappealing wedge of sweetened cream cheese. Was this what Bogart meant by "mucilage"?

This is Rivera's recipe according to Marti Buckley's cookbook, *Basque Country:*

Ingredients

1¾ c. (350 g.) sugar

2¼ lbs cream cheese at room temperature

¼ tsp. kosher salt

5 large eggs

2 c. (480 ml.) heavy cream (sometimes called heavy whipping cream)

¼ c. (30 g.) all-purpose flour

Directions

Take out the cream cheese early to let it soften.

Preheat the oven to 400 degrees.

Grease a springform pan and then line it with parchment paper. Press on the folds of the paper so that it lines the inside of the pan evenly.

Cream the sugar and cream cheese together with a mixer until smooth. Add the salt, and then the eggs, one by one, with the mixer. Then add the cream with a whisk. Sift in the flour.

Pour into the parchment-lined pan and put in the oven. Bake for 50 minutes. Check on it at 50 minutes. The top will be brown and the center jiggly. The addition of even one, two or three minutes will make a difference in the consistency of the cake and the thickness of the outside layer that holds the cake together. You can choose to let it cook a couple minutes more or less, but I promise, it will be delicious.

From Farther East

"Basque cheesecake" is also popular in Japan. Neither cheese, cream cheese, dairy, nor desserts in general are in the Japanese tradition. But in recent years, sweet shops have popped up in all the cities to follow different dessert fads. For a dessert to be trendy in Japan, it needs to have a foreign origin. After all, dessert is a foreign idea. For a time, everyone had to have cream puffs. Then there was baumkuchen, "tree cake," a German cake made on a spit. It had been eaten in Japan since 1919 but became a craze a century later. Then came Japanese cheesecake, fuwa-fuwa. Cheesecake has been a symbol of modern progress since 1868 when the Meiji emperor modernized and industrialized Japan. He introduced Western ideas, including foreign foods, because "Western" meant progress. An 1873 Japanese cookbook on modern cooking gave a recipe for cheesecake, but it was made from cheese and rice and was not really the Western idea of the cake. Like so many Western things in Japan, the Japanese had their own variation. But this one was not popular.

During the occupation of Japan after World War Two, American soldiers introduced many American foods, including New York cheesecake. This cheesecake, although an appealing idea, did not suit Japanese taste either, and Japanese bakers revised it. New York's was too sweet and too heavy, so they folded whipped egg whites into the batter and made it much lighter. Fuwa-fuwa is more a soufflé than a cake. Since the 1990s, fuwa-fuwa has become enormously popular, with two chains selling it throughout Japan. It is also sold in bakeries and cafés. And there are companies selling it in other countries, including the United States.

Tetsushi Mizokami was the son of owners of a bakery in Hakata, Japan. In 1995 he opened Uncle Tetsu, which specializes in Japanese cheesecake with outlets around the world including in the United States and Canada. Without giving out any secrets, Uncle Tetsu gives the vague outline of a recipe. He says there are six ingredients: cream cheese, milk, eggs, sugar, flour, and love. He does not specify the quantity of any of these, including the last.

I would suggest 250 grams cream cheese, about 60 grams softened butter, 100 ml whole milk, six eggs, about 70 grams flour, and 120 grams sugar. [Note: Careful not to overdo sugar.]

1. Create a smooth batter with cream cheese, butter, milk, egg yolks, and flour. [Note: I suggest beating them together in a mixer with a paddle attachment and in the order given.]

2. Whip egg whites and sugar together carefully to create the perfect meringue. [Note: I suggest using a whip attachment. Begin with whites and gradually whip in the sugar until it creates soft peaks. This means the meringue will form peaks but the tips will slightly fall over. In other words, not completely stiff.]

3. The two parts are brought together for the first time and poured into lightweight pans which are themselves set in a bath of water. [Note: Not so fast. The meringue has to be folded into the batter, which takes considerable skill. A portion of meringue is placed in the batter and the batter is gently folded over the meringue. Then more is added and carefully folded. This continues until a homogenous fluffy batter is

created. At no point is there to be any mixing or stir-
ring. It is very gently poured into the pans, the tops are
leveled with a rubber spatula, and an edge is created
around the top with the spatula handle.] Then the pans
are gently placed in a large pan of water. Bake in a low
oven, about 350 Fahrenheit, for 90 minutes. Then turn
off the oven and let slightly cool in the oven before
taking out. [Note: Removal from the pan becomes
much easier if you use springforms. Sometimes apricot
jam is spread on the warm top.]

ACKNOWLEDGMENTS

Thank you to my neighbor Gary Greengrass and to Herb Grosinger for their advice, and to my friend Yoko Clark for advice on Japan. Thanks to my thoughtful agent and wise adviser, Danielle Svetcov, to my editor, Hattie LeFavour, and especially the great Nancy Miller, dear friend with whom I have done twenty-something books.

A NOTE ON THE AUTHOR

MARK KURLANSKY is the *New York Times* bestselling author of *The Unreasonable Virtue of Fly Fishing*, *Milk!*, *Havana*, *Paper*, *The Big Oyster*, *1968*, *Salt*, *The Basque History of the World*, *Cod*, and *Salmon*, among other titles. He has received the Dayton Literary Peace Prize, *Bon Appétit*'s Food Writer of the Year Award, the James Beard Award, and the Glenfiddich Award. He lives in New York City.

www.markkurlansky.com